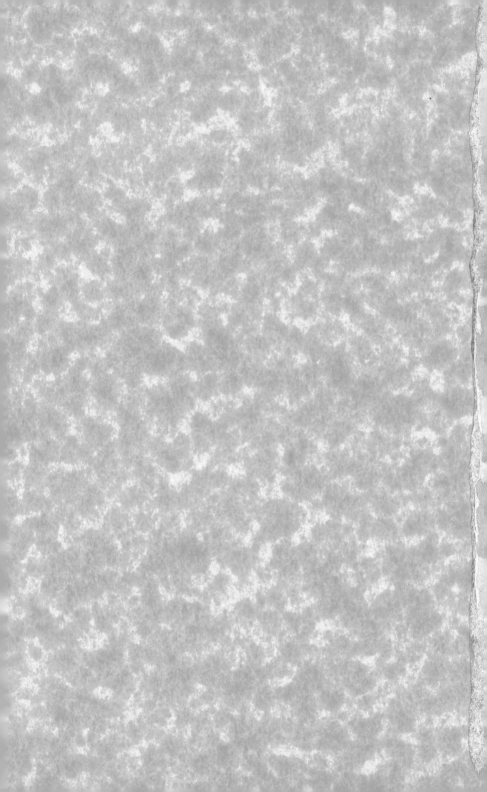

MINESWEEPER

I've come to accept that a fine beach with fine surf is going to be loved by lots of people.

You know who does not love it, though? Ma. Ma hates the ocean and the surfing and all that goes along with it, in the same way that seals must hate orcas. Even though surf life poses no threat to her happiness in the way that orcas do to seals.

"Where are you going, Fergus?" Ma said one day in June 1949. She said it wearily, as tired of this pointless exchange as I was.

I didn't even turn. I stood at the front door, having come so close to getting through it without this challenge. I sighed and talked to the door, to Ma. "You know where I'm going. The sun's out. It's hot and breezy. Conditions are perfect. My board is strapped onto the back of my truck for Pete's sake. Do you actually *like* having this talk? It gets us to the same exact non-place every time, and neither one of us ever seems to understand anything better by the end."

I truly didn't intend to be nasty to her. Every time I did it, I felt sorry. I coulda, shoulda done better, especially this time.

And yet every time I *felt* sorry, I failed to *say* that I was sorry.

"You are *so* like your father," she said.

This was a theme. A tireless, relentless theme.

"Good for him," I said, not for the first time.

I loved her. I felt bad for her, and I felt pain for her. I was almost certain that she could have said those exact same things about me. So why couldn't we manage to do better?

I love to surf. I used to love to do other things, like baseball and basketball and homework. Until I found surfing and it found me. I also love diving and snorkeling, but they're just offshoots of surfing. In service *to* surfing. I'll go underwater only when the overwater isn't worth the time, because the waves are not happening. You can figure out a lot about how waves behave by studying what's going on underneath them. The geography and rock formations, the channels between them, sandbars and shelves, they all come into play when shaping a wave. It's like a moving sculpture, that thing that forms on the surface and then delivers the great, crazy ocean from out there to crash onto the shoreline. There is a whole culture of waves that goes on beneath them. To understand surf you have to understand the unseen bits below. Waves want to be understood. They want somebody like me to pay attention to them.

CHRIS LYNCH

SPECIAL FORCES

MINESWEEPER

BOOK 2

SCHOLASTIC PRESS ★ NEW YORK

Library of Congress Cataloging-in-Publication Data available

ISBN 978 0 545 86165 6
10 9 8 7 6 5 4 3 2 1   19 20 21 22 23
First edition, December 2019

Printed in the U.S.A.   23
Book design by Christopher Stengel

CHAPTER ONE
A Graduation

My name is Fergus Frew Junior. Fergus Senior is dead. He was thirty-four years old in 1943 when he went to the bottom of the Atlantic Ocean and stayed there. I was twelve. It was the war. The big war. And Dad was bold and brave and ready and willing and able and all that stuff that makes people go googly over what our good guys did to wipe out the bad guys. He was heroic.

My ma has a theory. I hate it when she has those. She believes that I'm attached to the sea because the sea took my father and I'm trying to take him back.

Truth is, if there's any connection between me and Dad and the sea—which there isn't—then it would be because I hope to give him a good smacking around for failing to keep his head above water when he should have.

The ocean has been generally better to me than it was to my old man. That's primarily because I stay on top of it when I need to and go underneath it when I choose to. Mutual respect is what connects the water and me.

You have to maintain the respect. Otherwise, you are wasted.

And why my ma's theory is so stupid: It suggests that I or anybody else can win something back from the sea. No, sirree. A tug-o'-war over my father's earthly remains with the ocean itself? I miss ya plenty, Dad, but that's a loser's game, and you didn't raise no loser.

And that is my tribute to my father.

What I most like to do in the salty cold waves is to surf them.

I am a surfer.

I don't, however, care very much for other surfers. It may be unreasonable, but if I had my way, it would be me and the waves and nobody else. It doesn't work that way, unfortunately. If you've got something as awesome as the ocean waves bobbing around, you can't expect that you'll be the only one who appreciates them. Awesomeness attracts. Otherwise it wouldn't be awesomeness.

Understanding it doesn't mean I have to be happy about it, though.

That's all I wanted to do that day I shut the door on my unhappy mother. I knew she was unhappy. Maybe she had every right to be. Didn't matter, or at least it didn't matter enough, as I strode to my truck, hopped in, and pulled out of our driveway.

I couldn't hear my mother crying. But I knew that's what she was doing.

That was my graduation day.

I wasn't a nice guy then. I wasn't a *bad* guy, but I had trouble caring. And I wanted to be left alone. So once I got in my truck—which I *loved*, proving that I wasn't without feelings altogether—I didn't look back, didn't look up to see my mother's sad face in the window. I got in gear, stared straight ahead, and gunned it for the beach.

Fifteen minutes later I was climbing out of the truck, inhaling the great Pacific breeze, and unstrapping my board. As I made the transition from biped to motorhead to aqua creature, I paused almost involuntarily to admire the vehicle that made it all possible. It had become a ritual, as significant to the whole exercise as waxing my board or paddling into the waves.

I bought the big clunky beast with the money I'd made from three summers of lifeguarding. It was a 1932 Plymouth pickup, which at one time must have been some shade of brown but was now almost uniformly rust colored from nose to tail. It had been left to decay for most of its life, which was only a year shorter than mine, and pre-owned three times before I came along. All three owners had been farmers, which would account for the noble wear and tear on the truck. As far as farmers were concerned a patina of rust is not decay, it's just life.

And death. Funny, or not so funny, since one of the distinguishing characteristics of the truck was its "suicide doors," which hinged in the back and were generally considered unsafe. The guy who sold it to me told me that the first owner actually *had* committed suicide, though not in the Plymouth itself. A pea farmer, he was beaten down by the Great Depression, then opted for the Great Alternative. The truck sat for a few years before his wife unloaded it. The second guy farmed lettuce— which is just a vast waste of agricultural space, if you ask me. He had a stroke. The truck sat again until Farmer Three came along and bought it. He farmed cucumbers, and the less said about them the better. He sold it to me after having it for a couple of years, because he just couldn't stand to drive around in a "skid mark of a vehicle" anymore.

I nicknamed the truck Lucky.

San Onofre is my home beach. It has it all, really: bluffs and cliffs, hiking trails, sandy calm beachfronts, and best of all, a variety of surf spots. And I have a home within my home beach. I love a spot called Trestles, for a number of reasons. First, it was named for the railroad bridge running right alongside it. Trains and beaches, can't be beat. Second, it has all kinds of geological arrangements under the water, including craggy rock reefs and placid, ever-shifting sand fields. They make the break inscrutable and alive and always new. Every time you surf Trestles, you have to figure it out all over again.

But possibly my favorite aspect of all is that, unlike the other San Onofre beaches, you have to park your vehicle and then haul your board nearly a mile down a nature trail just to reach Trestles, passing under said trestle and through a wetland full of nutty bird-watchers.

I love bird-watchers. I don't care much for their hobby, but they bother absolutely nobody while doing it.

About surfing and surfers, I feel precisely the opposite. Nothing gets in a surfer's way like other surfers.

Because of all these conditions, and it being graduation day across the county, I came to the clearing onto Trestles to find I had the place pretty much to myself. This, I have to say, was my paradise.

I was almost *too* excited as I started running toward the ocean, my board tucked under my arm. I'd forgotten how much of a strain walking from the car with my board always was. I stumbled, as awkwardly as a fit young man with a board can stumble, fighting the inevitable until I finally fell to the warm ground. Before making it twenty yards into the run, I'd hurtled shoulder-first, bouncing off my own board and leaving a mask of my stupid face in the sand.

I got up quickly, brushing myself down and looking around desperately for any witnesses. Seagulls came from all over to swoop and squawk and laugh their beaky heads off at me.

"Fine," I said, gathering up the board and resuming a more dignified pace toward the waves, "just don't tell anybody."

I slapped down on the water and took my time paddling out. This was a day. I could feel the chilly water on my hands and feet, lapping up over the sides of the board and licking my torso, while at the same time the midday sun warmed my bare back. I had on my long shorts, cut off just below the knees, and by the time I'd gotten out past the break they were sodden. It was a good feeling.

I was in no rush. Once past the break I hoisted myself onto the board and floated for a bit. I spread my arms wide and looked up into the sky, letting the sunshine melt over me and wash down into the water. There was a nice roll to the surf, though nothing too urgent. I watched the empty beach with satisfaction, like the whole place was mine. Surfers could be a territorial bunch, especially around here, which was one reason I never warmed up to them much. It always seemed beyond stupid to me, to get possessive over something so great and unpossessable as a whole mighty ocean.

Unless it was like this. Just myself and the swells of salty water. Nobody in sight. Nobody to laugh at me but the seagulls, and they had nobody to tell. I stared, satisfied that the beach was empty of people and would remain that way, which was a blissful state of affairs. A guy could be forgiven for feeling like such a vision belonged to him. You're not hogging something to yourself if there is nobody else present to hog it from, right?

It's when other people show up that everything gets messy.

With a couple of gentle right-hand strokes through the water, my board reoriented itself seaward and I had turned my back to the land. I drifted my mind across the far horizon, and my mind was quite happy to be there.

My classmates were probably all lining up at the entrance to the auditorium about now. I felt a pang. I didn't want to be at graduation, but the pang did not seem to know that.

Then, Ma's face. Her voice came skimming to me across the surface of the water just as a big swell came under me, followed by a bigger one still. Her voice was sad, and the swells roiled under me and up through me, and I did not like that.

I turned my back on the distant horizon and faced inland again. I heard her clearly this time, a sigh, a depleted whoosh of a sound that urged me into paddling before I even knew why.

The wave knew, though. From an easy paddle I suddenly found myself windmilling into an insistent wave that had snuck up from the middle of the ocean. As it arched like a big watery cat waking from a nap, I found myself whirling away with powerful strokes, then jumping to my feet to join with this feisty nine-foot wave.

I caught it, caught the leading edge and leaned into it. I was whipping along the ridge of the beautiful thing, this gift from somewhere, and I could just tell as I pushed hard on my back foot that this beast couldn't throw me if it tried.

Except that it did. As magically as the great wave had arrived, it produced one enormous buck that tossed me in the air. I hit the water with my chest, then went under.

I felt my board kick away to my left, just before another, bigger wave came up over the top of the last. I scrambled to get to the surface and had just about cracked it when a fourth unfriendly breaker broke right over my face and shoulders and drove me back under. I went over backward, feeling the salty water force its way into my sinuses before I finally corkscrewed up in time for the last of the waves to deposit me onto the packed sand.

I sat for a few minutes, wondering where all that had come from. The surf around here is known to be just unpredictable enough for a constant challenge, but it's not known to be as surly as that.

The spot where I'd landed was a lucky one, no more than ten yards from a bank of nasty-looking rocks that would have been no fun at all to get acquainted with. I was surprised to find myself there, as I had started in a position relative to the surf that shouldn't have left me anywhere near this. My board knew better and was just now bobbing to a near stop on a far more accommodating bit of beach nearly forty yards along the water's edge from me.

I took the long, slow walk to retrieve it and eased my way back into the face of the rolling waves.

Again, as I paddled I encountered nothing too rough. In fact, the surf was calm enough that if it didn't improve, the afternoon would be something of a washout. But I knew this place well enough not to count it out so soon.

Once out far enough beyond the break, I settled into floating some more. If nothing else, my tan was going to have a good day today. Which could not be said for all the unfortunates in flat hats stuck in the school auditorium at the same time. It was probably mid-ceremony by now. I was glad not to be putting my mother through that tedium. Proud, even. What a fine son.

The quiet was getting to me. I felt, then saw, a promising, juicy swell coming to collect me. This time I paddled hard and furious like I was intending to steam into port under Fergus power, rather than surf. But the wave had more moxie than I'd realized, because it caught up to me before I made it to my feet. Recovering with a burst, I hopped into position in time to find myself on the crest of a beauty. I felt like one of those rodeo trick riders, standing on the back of a brute of a galloping runaway horse.

The wave grabbed me up and took charge, seeming to change its very direction as it whipped me right and left, while slinging me straight forward at the same time. At its maximum height it must have reached twelve feet, but the maximum lasted a blink before somebody yanked the cord. I descended like I was a roasted chicken rushing downstairs in a dumbwaiter. There was a loud *plop-slap* sound as my board landed flat on the low water at the bottom of the broken wave.

Then there was nothing. The rush ended so quickly that it left me standing there, floating on my board in calm, shallow water, as if I had not surfed a big, angry wave at all.

It was a completely strange sensation, standing on the board in the shallows. This was not how a ride ended. You rode it in or more likely you crashed it out. But this? It felt as if the surf had been entirely withdrawn. A carpet yanked from underfoot and rolled away.

I turned, still standing, out toward the horizon once more. The water all around me, the whole ocean, it seemed, was smooth as a pudding that had set. There was a hint of a ripple emanating from the edges of my board, and lisping liquid sounds came from it.

I did not care for this.

I felt like I could hear my mother again. Not words, but her voice. And the kids in my class. Their feet marching up under flowing robes to collect their diplomas, then marching back again surrounded by the smiling faces of everybody important to them. Those sounds were clearer to me than anything I could sense in the real world. Except the wicked seagulls, suddenly consumed with buzzing and laughing at me again.

I jumped off my board, kicking it out from under me and sending it scooting onto the beach. All that, I could hear. I could also hear myself marching, one and two and three and four *plop-splash*es, launching myself into the air and crashing through the surface of the water.

Into proper silence.

In the absence of any decent wave action, the only job worth doing now was to dive and explore and demand some answers.

Like nature owes me or anybody else answers.

I dove and started swimming in the direction of the choppiest, rockiest section of the beach. The part where I nearly landed on the rocks. The water was as clear as it gets, so I could see wonderfully well as I neared the stony formations. Nothing unusual appeared, compared to the many times I'd explored this water world in the past. There were highs and lows among the rocks, tunnels, and small caves. There were sections of virgin sand spread like carpet on the ocean floor, and then something more like tiling. Broad, flat stones laid themselves out as neatly as a paved driveway.

There were currents competing and slipping past one another. Different depths gave you different currents, different temperatures, different pressures. It was one of the most interesting aspects of the surf. Of all the many explorations I had made down here to date, no two were ever remotely alike. But none were ever wasted, either. I didn't understand it entirely, but every scouting trip I made somehow stamped itself into my brain, which stored all of it into an ever expanding sense of what was under my board when I awaited the wave.

I swam farther through the rocks, down under the archways. I was just about to enter a cave when, *sheesh*, I pulled up and jumped back, coming very nearly in nose contact with a good-size—bad-size—eel. I immediately started retreating, whirring away backward like a giant aquatic hummingbird, until I was convinced he wanted nothing more from me than to get away to his private hidey-hole.

With pleasure. I didn't normally fear eels or anything else I encountered underwater. As long as I had a little warning, I was fine. One of the many great things about ocean life as I'd found it was that things seemed to run on a live-and-let-live basis when it came to human visitation. Don't pose a threat, don't receive a threat is basically how it worked.

Fine by me.

It was about time for me to surface anyway. I wasn't finding any conclusive evidence to the surf's mood today, and I had reached just about my limit. It was one of my prouder claims, that after all my time in the water the past few years, I could now dive and stay under for nearly three minutes. I had no watch on—I was dying to get a proper diver's watch someday—but my lungs were reading about two minutes fifty.

When I broke the surface, breaching like a tiny whale, I found the surf was surprisingly feisty again. I'd sensed none of this from beneath, which was rare. I just couldn't quite get a handle on things today, and so it seemed prudent to clear out. I wasn't superstitious, like a lot of surfers were, but I wasn't silly, either. And I had respect.

I swam back, around the rock reef, steaming across

the last stretch of wave water, then beached myself and got to my feet. I went to collect my board.

But my board was not available for collection.

There was still nobody else on the beach. I looked up and down the waterline, then up and down the shallows, then up and down the not-so-shallows in case the tide had sucked my board back. Nothing doing. The seagulls started, on cue, to laugh at me again. They were so focused on it that I briefly thought they may have been involved in the disappearance.

Of course, that was crazy. But that was how quickly I was becoming frantic over this. My board had become my best friend over the last couple of years, and the thought of losing it made me just as edgy as having it made me relaxed.

The truth, it turned out, was even crazier than the delusion. Seagulls famously never did anything helpful for anybody, but here they were, circling and squawking over me, then over the water in a more or less straight shot in front of me, then to another point on the horizon where they circled once more over something.

That something was a surfboard. Quite possibly my surfboard, since there was no one else in the vicinity.

Except that there was a somebody out there. Sitting on the board, apparently awaiting waves to catch.

I sprinted back into the water and launched myself like a torpedo. Swimming so hard and fast I swear I must have been making outboard motor noises, I crashed straight through several oncoming waves. When I finally emerged on the far side of the break, I started screaming at the guy.

"What do you think you're doing?"

He paused, as if he had to translate my words in his head.

"I think I'm floating."

I was already angrier.

"But what are you floating *on*?"

He looked downward. Then back up at me. "A surfboard."

Swimming and shouting simultaneously is harder than you might think. But I tore into both with everything I had.

"Not *a* surfboard," I hollered. "*My* surfboard!"

He bobbed up and down on the swells, just another buoy in the bay. "Is it?"

"Yes!"

"'Cause I just found it. It was right over there—"

"I know where it was," I bellowed, "because I left it there."

"Oh," he said calmly as I approached the board— *my* board. "Thanks."

"*No*, not thanks," I said, grabbing on to the board and hoisting myself onto it so that the guy and I were sitting, squared up, our knees bumping. "Not thanks. And not welcome. If you knew anything about surfing, you'd know you do not ever touch another person's board. There's no *finding* a board lying on the beach, there's just *stealing* a board from the beach."

"Okay, okay," he said, trying to calm me down with his soothing surfer tone. "Okay, so I didn't find it. But I didn't steal it, either. I just borrowed it. I knew where you were the whole time. I saw you go in the water. I knew you'd be back. Unless you drowned under there or something. In which case you wouldn't have any need for a surfboard. Waste not, want not, right?"

"No way were you on the beach when I went in," I said.

"Um, I think I was."

"I looked all over, and I didn't see you at all. I'd never miss something like that."

He shrugged. "Well, you missed me. And hey, you stayed under a really long time. You some kind of merman or something?"

I was still tense, and my voice and body language were showing it. There we were, bobbing on the surface of the great Pacific, two guys—two total strangers—sitting face-to-face on one board. One sacred board, and I was not making that up. You do *not* mess with another surfer's stuff. Everybody who isn't a jerk or a knucklehead knows that.

"So," I said, "are you a jerk or a knucklehead?"

This didn't appear to bother him as much as I'd hoped it would.

"Depends on who you ask," he said.

"I'm asking *you*," I said, probably unnecessarily. This whole episode was riling me up something fierce. More than I would have expected it to. The sacred nature of surfing rules is real and meaningful, but I didn't like to think of myself as one of those line-in-the-sand kind of guys. Normally I was pretty slow to anger, so this feeling, this day, was kind of surprising me. And the fact that I was caught so off guard was putting me even more on edge.

"Then I'm gonna go with knucklehead," the guy said cheerily.

Which of course just made me more irritated. I'd had enough.

He was fairly fit, his pectorals looking like they were carved out of brown slate. And when I jabbed a finger into one of them, that's what it felt like, too.

"Get off my board," I growled.

He got visibly less cheery. Not angry, but not friendly, either.

"I was planning on riding it back in," he said evenly. "Then you can have it back. Funny thing is, I don't much like swimming. Strange, right, for a surf—"

Couldn't tell if he saw it coming. I couldn't have cared less, either. Because he should have.

With a quick and snappy open-hand swat, I belted him sideways. He started falling over to his right, then caught himself by catching me. He clamped on to both my elbows and dragged me awkwardly down into the water with him.

With the water still so clear, I got a good look at him as we exchanged our first submerged kicks and punches. He tried the "hands up, let's stop" gesture quickly enough to boost my confidence tremendously. It was already fairly high, since one of the last things he'd said up topside was how he wasn't big on swimming. And I, apparently, was a merman.

I took several more shots through his defenses, but with it being underwater and all, it was less like punching and more like pushing with fists.

This went on for what seemed like a long time but couldn't have been more than a few seconds. Time itself goes slower when you're submerged. But we both knew how this was going to end, slate pecs or no slate pecs. It could have been Rocky Marciano grappling with me down there; nobody was going to outlast me underwater.

The guy was well aware of it, too. He might have been a knucklehead, but he wasn't stupid. He'd very quickly depleted his oxygen by flailing around and trying to tie me up. But I just bopped him several times on the nose, the way they say you should defend yourself against a shark. Finally, he made his move. He got both hands on top of my head and shoved me downward. Then he got his feet on my shoulders and with one great kick managed to send me toward the bottom while propelling himself up to the top.

At first I reacted with fury, paddling madly toward his kicking feet, hoping to pull him back into the fray.

Then I thought: *No, I'll show him.* I stopped swimming altogether. I just let myself go, drifting casually toward the surface. I was in no hurry to suck in air like he was, and in every hurry to show that I didn't need to. If he would have muscles, I would have lungs.

I was even enjoying the view, as I came within about six feet of the surface. I watched him flailing around, toward my board, then clamber up onto it. Very satisfying to me.

Until he started windmilling, and the board started skimming toward shore. Then it scooted really quickly, and I raced to the surface.

I was just in time to catch him catching it, a big horse-necked beauty of a curling wave. He hit it just right, too, riding the crest, zigging along it until zagging was required to extend the ride. He had great control, despite the wave being big and powerful and my board being built more for speed than control.

I watched, first in fury, then eventually with envy, as the guy on my board enjoyed a wave like I hadn't enjoyed in months. He was good, and aware of it.

So he was a knucklehead *and* a jerk.

It was one of the longest swims of my life. And I'd been in long-distance swimming competitions.

"I can't help thinking we've met someplace before," the guy said as I crawled out of the surf like the last survivor of a shipwreck. He was sitting cross-legged in the sand, with my board lying right alongside him like a loyal dog. Traitor board.

"Go ahead," I said, "enjoy your moment. You earned it."

"I will. And I did." No taking the high road for this guy.

"Thought you'd have skedaddled before I got out," I said.

"Well," he said, "I thought about it, but then I figured that would be rude, after you loaned me your rig and everything. Also, I've had nothing but laughs since I met you. How many people can you say that about?"

I did not respond to that in any way.

I sat down in the sand next to him, looking out at the ocean and the decent roll of the waves.

"What's your name?" he asked me after a few peaceful minutes.

I answered his simple, straightforward question the same way I would have when I was six. "What's *your* name?"

"Duke," he said, making it easy. Making me look stupid. Which is also easy.

"Fergus," I said finally.

"Huh?" Duke said.

"Fergus. That's my name."

"Oh. Caught me off guard there. Fergus. Sounds like the kind of thing you say after somebody sneezes."

I rose slowly, mightily, to my feet. "You want to go again?" I said, fists balled at my sides, towering over him.

He smiled up at me, as pleased as if I'd just offered him a bite of my candy apple.

"Okay, if you insist," he said. "But we ain't in the water anymore, Fergus. And this is a United States Marine you're calling to arms." He held his hands out in front of him the way you would if you were about to commence playing the piano. They were big. Gnarled. Not piano hands.

"I suppose I could be a little friendlier," I said, thinking better of it, and corkscrewed artfully back into my seat. I took his great right paw into my human-scaled hand and gave it a shake.

"That's the way," Duke said, shaking enthusiastically. "And if you were friendlier, you might not be so friendless."

"What?" I said, letting his hand drop. "How do you . . . You don't know that!"

He raised his hands in phony surrender. "You're right, you're right, I don't know. It's just, you don't seem to have many social skills."

Perhaps unwisely, I rose to my feet again. "You know, Duke, there will come a point where I'll have to risk having you pound me into the sand . . ."

Now he laughed out loud and clapped those major mitts together. The sound was like a rifle shot. It skimmed out across the water and probably didn't stop until it reached Japan.

"I gotta tell you," he said, grabbing my hand and pulling me back down, "with comedy skills like those, it's hard to believe you have no friends."

I turned sharply toward him. He shrank away from me like he was terrified. He wasn't. But he wasn't done, either.

"Okay, I'll do it," he said with a pinch of mock desperation. "I'll be your friend if you quit trying to fight me."

Even I could see a good deal when it was presented to me.

"See, Duke, this is why I don't usually bother having any friends. You all stink."

"Ha!" he said, punching me on the shoulder hard enough to tip me all the way over.

When the next ten minutes went by without another word, I started thinking that we had already exhausted all conversational possibilities. But silence between people, I realized, could be its own sort of conversation.

"Marines, huh?" I said, when I'd had my fill of it.

"Yup. Stationed at Camp Pendleton just up the road. You local?"

"Yeah. Born and raised in the boringest town on Earth, San Clemente."

"Ah, I'm sure it's not that bad."

"It is. It's so bad I'm already bored with talking about it. Where are you from?"

"Hawaii."

I nearly jumped to my feet again, though this time for less combative reasons.

"Hawaii?" I said. "I've been dying to go there for practically my whole life! It must be rotten to get stuck here after living in Hawaii."

"No."

"No? Why no?"

"Don't get me wrong, it's a beautiful place. Every bit as nice as the postcards say. It's not the island's fault . . . It's probably mine. A surfer's paradise, as you may have heard."

"I surely have. That's one reason I've been dying to go. I want to experience it for myself. Makaha, Waimea, those places are legendary!"

"And their legends are well-earned. It is indeed a surfer's paradise, if it wasn't for one big drawback."

I kind of thought he might finish that thought on his own. But after a quiet minute or so I figured I was entitled to ask.

"That drawback being . . . ?"

"Surfers. Thing is, I love surf, love surfing. It's surfers I can't stand."

I couldn't believe this. I felt like the last dodo coming across another dodo.

"That's exactly how I feel!" I said. "It's like they think they own the whole world. Or at least one small, kind of fantastic corner of it. You'd think they would be happy enough to just be in such a great spot, doing such a great thing . . . But they seem so interested in making it *watch me, watch me*, like a bunch of peacocks. And being all possessive and territorial, as if the surf is something that can be *owned* by anybody."

"Exactly. And if you think it's bad here, try to imagine how *infested* Hawaii is with those guys. That's partly why I stole your board . . . I assumed you were one of them."

"I knew it!" I said. "I knew you had every intention to be a jerk."

"Guilty," Duke said, kind of apologetic, kind of proud.

"Okay, so, you joined the service to escape Hawaii? You've got to be the first guy ever to do that."

"No, no, you got it wrong. Since the war ended and they sent all the guys who did the dirty work home, military service is a cushy deal. There's nobody left to fight, but plenty of bases that need to be staffed. And since they went and used up all the prime fighting-age population, they'll take you as long as you have an inclination and a pulse. You get to see the world, develop a specialty . . . It can be a nice, safe living."

"I have a pulse," I said. "But I have no such inclination. For one thing, my dad was killed in the war."

"So what? So was mine. I figure that's just all the more reason they owe us an easy living in nice surroundings."

"Hmm," I said. "I don't think it's healthy to go around thinking that anybody owes me anything. Especially just because my father died."

"Well, you should reconsider that thinking. Was your father a Marine?"

"No."

"Navy? 'Cause you are a natural water baby."

"No. He was Army. Special Forces. Devil's Brigade. Although he did die in the water. Part of a combined services operation."

"Well, you swim like some kind of natural amphibian. You should be headed toward one of the water services, for sure."

"I'm not headed anywhere, Duke. Didn't the whole military just sort of shut down when the war ended?"

"Nah, they didn't shut it down. Reduced it in size, though. Still have to man bases all over the world. It's a career now rather than an obligation. Plus the benefits. The Marine Corps is going to pay for college once I'm done."

"Well, good for you," I said, winding down this segment of the Duke and Fergus show. "I should probably get going." I stood and reached for my board, but Duke got there first, picked it up, and started walking toward the path to the parking lot.

"You going this way?" he asked.

"Yeah," I said, "but you don't have to carry that."

"Consider it my bill. For renting your board."

I had just been about to take it from him, or at least insist he let me help, when I remembered his unauthorized *rental*.

"Sure," I said, following behind him up the path. "Why not?"

When we had hiked the mile back to the parking area and I pointed out my car, Duke's reaction was, "Really?"

"Really," I echoed. "What's not to believe?"

"It's not disbelief. I'm impressed. I mean, it could certainly use a paint job. Are those suicide doors?"

"Yup," I said proudly. "And I can even top that. The original owner committed suicide, reportedly."

"Did the doors play any part in it?"

"Not that I'm aware of."

"Still, haunted truck. Sort of impressive."

I took the board off him and began strapping it in the bed. "It's a good truck, anyway," I said. But as I turned toward him again he'd already started down the footpath toward the beach. "Nice to meet you!" I called.

He turned but kept walking backward. "Same to you."

"Guess I'll see you around," I said.

"Guess you will," he said. "Can't miss me, really. Any time I'm off duty I'm probably here. Hiking the bluffs, walking the trails, bird-watching, body surfing . . ."

"Then I guess you *will* be hard to miss," I said.

"So don't try." Then he signed off with an exaggeratedly big wave.

By the time I finally got home, the house was completely quiet. Ma didn't greet me the way she normally did, asking me how the surf was and all that, even though she couldn't have cared less. The place smelled strongly of two things: meat loaf and tears.

My mother's crying had a powerful scent, for as long as I could remember. She smelled like the sea when she cried, which was more often than anyone should have to.

I loved her meat loaf to an indecent degree.

I walked into the kitchen to find a tray of it on the table. It was still warm, wrapped in foil on top of a napkin. *Happy Graduation, Son* was written on the foil in blue ink.

I sat down in front of the loaf.

"Thank you!" I yelled up to the ceiling, in the general direction of her bedroom.

There was no response, but I hadn't anticipated one. I hadn't anticipated the meat loaf, either. I lay my head down lightly on the metallic foil, absorbing the warmth and wondering what was wrong with me, why I couldn't do better for Ma.

I needed a shower, though, so even the meat loaf was going to have to wait.

It was good enough to wait for, and it would still be pretty warm by the time I settled in with a knife and fork, some ketchup, and nothing else. A whole lot of nothing else.

Why could I not do better? She deserved better.

CHAPTER TWO

Lost and Aimless

I spent my summer after high school pretty much the same way I spent the summer before, and the one before that. I surfed when I could and put in my hours as a lifeguard on the beach to keep the Plymouth filled up with gas and my belly filled up with hot dogs and ice cream.

I swam a lot, too. I always swam a lot, but swimming and diving felt more like my natural state of being than ever before. Water experiences were becoming the only experiences I felt any passion for whatsoever. Beyond that, I was spending much more time exploring the depths of the blue Pacific than skimming over the surface of it. The deeper the better.

I wanted to be alone.

And there is no alone like beneath-the-surface alone. No matter how many other people are under the water with you or sailing over your head. No matter how many crabs and eels and jellyfish you encounter while you are down there. When you have the ocean wrapped tightly around your skull, nothing else can get to you.

And that is a sensational sensation.

Sometimes, though, I couldn't quite manage to reach the water before someone else snagged me. Sometimes, there was interference.

"Fergus?" came the now-familiar call as I raced toward the beach. "Fergus, where you off to? Wait up."

It was Duke. It was always Duke.

I stopped, turned to see him running my way. Behind me was the ocean. I gestured toward it.

"I'm going there, Duke. Into the water. Like usual. There's nothing else in that direction. Where else would I be going?"

"Jeez," he said as we both continued to the shore, "somebody woke up on the wrong side of Wednesday."

But the thing was, he seemed untroubled by my mood. He was never troubled by my mood. I wouldn't have minded if once in a while he *was* troubled by my mood.

"I'll tell you what," Duke said, just before I submerged. "You love water like nobody's business."

"I'll tell you what else," I responded. "It *is* nobody's business."

And with that, I dove.

Sometimes, it seemed, I was inclined to treat Duke the same way I treated my mother. Neither one deserved it. In fact, at this point it was probably fair to say they were my two favorite people in the world.

Unfortunately, that wasn't such a hotly contested title.

But my truest friends were the waves. Boulders, seaweed, fish, crustaceans. Bivalves. My truck. My board.

Things that didn't talk to me.

These were the times when I valued my free-diving abilities most. Nobody could keep up with me. It was a powerful feeling, actually. If I wanted to—needed to—I could just evaporate from the dry, boring world. I could do it, and nobody could do anything about it.

This day, it seemed like I was breaking some kind of record for staying under. It seemed, in fact, like there was no limit to how long I could last. I went down and down, swam with the sea life, swam *as* sea life. I wove in and out of rock formations, skimming the scraggly bottom of the bay with my chest. I disturbed schools of fish, caused crabs to scuttle, and just generally absorbed the very aquatic essence of what this world had to offer.

To be alone in the vastness of the ocean was to be magnificently alone.

I was aware of the mundane world slipping away behind me, the families enjoying the Southern California perfection, the beach bums posing and lounging mightily on the sand and along the water's edge like basking seals. I knew everything here because when I was not enjoying it, I was patrolling it as a lifeguard, scanning the surf with my hawklike stare, my whistle, and my tiny paddleboard.

Not today, though. Today I was off. Off duty, off the map, and off the land in my soaking, silent paradise.

Whenever I dove, all I could think of was diving some more.

Is that not a pretty good definition of heaven?

Except, of course, it never could last.

"How *do* you do that?" Duke said when I eventually surfaced and he swam out to meet me two hundred yards offshore. He was huffing hard with the effort of it.

I could never shake him for long. Duke didn't have my diving prowess, but he was more of a sea eagle than I was. Like a bird of prey circling overhead, he had the ability to track me no matter where I swam, no matter how fast or how deep.

"Like this," I said, breaching like a dolphin to dive once more with my newly refilled lungs.

The last thing I heard before going under was his great, complaining, "Awwww."

I actually laughed under the water.

I couldn't help but like the guy. He was funny and warm and good company.

If you liked that kind of thing.

I just didn't like that kind of thing enough to stay topside.

Had to give him credit for persistence, though. After spending the whole morning diving, swimming, exploring, surfacing, and diving some more, I returned to shore to find Duke sitting cross-legged, waiting for me in the sunshine. Just as I had expected.

"Brought you lunch," I said as I approached him. I presented one large and lovely crab with my right hand, and a hearty stalk of slick broad-leaf seaweed with the other.

"You probably don't think I'll eat this meal," he said, examining them both like a connoisseur.

"I probably wouldn't doubt it for a second," I said.

It was like that. *He* was like that; I was like that; we were like that, all through that summer. Depending on what the Marines had him doing on any given day, Duke would just show up, or not. At the family beach, where I was on duty as a lifeguard. At Trestles, where I would go to surf and dive on my days off.

It was effortless for him to track me, wherever I was.

Sometimes, he was even waiting for me when I pulled up in my truck.

"Let's do something different today," he said on one of those days. He talked as if we made plans, ever, rather than just kind of stumbling across each other.

"Why would we want to do that?" I said, sitting in the cab of the parked truck and gesturing out the open window toward the more open sky. The sun was beating down on us like a vendetta. Even by the standards of hot Southern California summers, this was some woozy-making heat.

"Change of pace, change of scenery, change of routine," he said with a triple shrug.

"What if none of those things appeal to me?" I asked, because none of those things appealed to me.

"Wouldn't you like to be fit as a Marine?" he asked. He pointed with one index finger toward himself and with the other toward the bluffs that lurked high above the beach. From our vantage, they didn't seem very far from the sizzling sun.

"Not really," I said, squinting dramatically upward.

Duke surprised me then. He turned right away from me and started hiking solo. "As you wish, Fergus. Your loss."

This was, naturally, perfectly okay with me. I couldn't even remember the last day when I didn't wake up thinking how pleased I was to be heading toward the water. And on days like this, even regular landlubber types came from all over the state, the country, the planet to indulge in the wet and wonderful gifts of San Onofre.

As I circled around the truck to begin unleashing my board, I found myself checking and then rechecking Duke's progress up the trail from the parking lot.

My loss. My loss? How could anything be my loss when one of the world's truly magical stretches of shoreline was waiting for me? I never wanted anything but this.

Except.

Except, lately, something had started foaming at the edges of my brain about the regularity of my days, my summer, and my life.

What was I doing? Where was I going? How long could I keep doing it? And where, if anywhere, was it getting me?

Duke was just coming to a bend in the trail where he'd curve around to the opposite, leeward side of the bluffs. Soon he would disappear from view.

Good. Nutty idea anyway.

Except. Again, except.

What was going on here? I had already spent most of my summer avoiding this odd and mysterious Marine. Now he was suggesting pulling me away from my beloved surf on the steamiest and laziest day off of the year so far.

There was no sense to it.

Nor to this.

I left the board tied right where it was and found myself trotting in the direction of that trail after . . . my *friend*?

I was already sweating before I turned around the bend in the trail. And on the other side there wasn't even a breeze.

"Hey!" I yelled, my voice carrying much better than it would have on the windward side of the bluffs.

He was a hundred yards or so up the trail already. He turned, grinned broadly, then spread his arms wide like we hadn't seen each other in years.

I was almost embarrassed, for both of us. More than almost.

He waited right there for me, his arms remaining outstretched. I jogged along because it was only polite not to keep him.

I slapped his arms down when I reached him. I couldn't help matching his goofy smile.

"Duke of *Delirium*," I said.

"Sure," he said. "Why not?"

He turned and resumed hiking. I followed right behind.

It didn't take long to understand why Duke was as fit as he was. This hill-climbing stuff was more grueling than it looked. When it came to climbing, Duke was every bit the equal of myself at free-diving.

And he could carry on conversation effortlessly at the same time.

"Did you see in the news?" he said, looking back over his shoulder while continuing to hike. "President Truman pulled the last of our troops out of South Korea. I told you, it's all going just like I said it would. The world is becoming a peace-loving place. No more wars. All we have to do is keep showing up, looking hard and hand-some, and the whole world will behave themselves. Because of what we did in the war. The war to end all wars, right?"

"Ugghh," I said, marching. Huffing and marching.

And sweating. It was a multipurpose *ugghh*, addressed to the sweltering, relentless sky and the degree of incline under my sneakered, sockless feet. There were almost certainly blisters in my near future. I was also responding to the topic of conversation, which was not at all new. Duke had been investing whatever spare time and breath he had into it for the past month, selling me on the idea of how perfect a military life would be for the likes of me. We even had drawn-out conversations about what "the likes of me" would be. Turned out that the likes of me were a lot like the likes of him, only with more-developed aquatic skills.

"What does that mean, Fergus? *Ugghh*? That mean you heard the news or didn't hear the news, or some other *ugghh* I don't understand?"

"I heard, Duke. In fact, I heard before you did. Truman called to ask what I thought before he made his decision."

"Really? Excellent. Did you mention my name? Tell him I'm a fan?"

"No need. He brought you up before I had a chance."

"Good man. Seriously, though. What are you going to do? You can't be a beach bum for the rest of your life."

"I'm a lifeguard."

"Lifeguarding is just beach bumming with a smaller board."

I was really sweating at this point. I was not used to this kind of perspiration. Whenever I got anywhere near this body temperature—which was not often—I found myself in the water within minutes. Problem solved.

"I'll be fine," I said.

"To be honest, you seem kind of lost. Aimless."

"My aim is generally pretty good," I said. "The ocean always turns up right where I left it. I've never missed yet."

"I used to be lost and aimless," he said. "So I know what it looks like."

We had reached the top of one headland, where I figured—hoped—we were going to stop for a spell. Apparently, though, Duke has favorites among promontories, so we kept going.

"We'll stop over there," he called as I fell off the pace. He pointed across to another cliff, one that looked suspiciously like the one we were already on. To get to it we'd have to make a jump Paul Bunyan couldn't have managed. That, or scramble down one steep cliff face and then up another. The third option would be walking a great U-shaped arc back toward inland and out once more to basically where we already were—only fifty feet or so north and equally close to the sun.

Duke passed me by on his way, retracing our recent steps. He patted me hard on the shoulder as he did.

"Whyyyy?" was the best I could do.

He let out a hearty one-syllable laugh. "We'll get you fighting fit yet," he said.

"Are you being paid to recruit people?" I asked as I fell in behind like a good soldier.

"Not at all. It's out of the goodness of my heart. My heart's goodness is also responsible for steering you in the direction of the Navy. If I had my druthers, you would be signed up and checked in alongside me in the Marines, stationed at Pendleton."

He let that one hang there in the baked air, as did I. We trekked along in silence, back inland, tacking northward, then turned around in the direction of the ocean once more. The only direction that ever makes any true sense anyway.

The sandstone that makes up the bluffs looks like it could crumble away if you jumped up and down on it with enough enthusiasm. If we really were Paul Bunyan and Babe the blue ox, we'd have been rolling into the water already. But we were on fairly solid ground as we made our way across the flat top of the cliff, through scrubby vegetation that wouldn't look out of place alongside the highway through Death Valley. I followed Duke to the very edge, where he sat, and then I sat, realizing for myself just what a majestic spot this was.

"Guess this answers my question of why," I said, perhaps unnecessarily.

"Guess this does," he said. Definitely unnecessarily.

The waves looked naturally smaller from here and farther away than these peaks looked from the beach. But they also looked broader, busier, and more a part of the great endless ocean than they ever could from sea level. I had hiked the bluffs a number of times, but for some reason, I never quite saw *this*.

"How come I never noticed all this?" I said, sweeping my arm in as much of a 360-degree arc as I could manage without twirling down the rock face.

"My guess?" Duke said, his gaze out in the middle distance. "Too much of a hurry."

I thought for a few seconds, trying to fix my stare at that same mid-distance.

And I thought, *He's just about right*. Even when I was in the rare mood for a hike, I was always desperate to get back to the waves. Even—no, especially—when I got to any of the bluff openings that presented and framed the sea so magically, my heart would start pounding and my feet would start shuffling, aching to get me back where I belonged.

"How do you know so much, Duke?"

I asked this as we soaked in the view and the sea-sky scent. The sea eagle seemed to know more than any human alive.

"That's the *only* thing I don't know," he said. "How it is that I know so much? I think about it a lot, and I just don't know. Drives me nuts, not knowing that."

I sighed loudly.

"Right," I said. "Ask a stupid question . . ."

He paused for several seconds, then pointed at me like he was just about to figure out a great truth.

"How does that end? I think I used to know it."

It was weeks before I saw Duke again, but during that time I spent a great deal of time thinking about the things he'd said. The summer continued to be picture-perfect. The surf was great, and hiking the bluffs was better now that I'd been shown how to do it right. It rained maybe three days the whole time, just enough to keep the vegetation viable. Even the bird-watching was a lot of fun, especially the way the birds seemed all brave and friendly right after the rains.

Except the seagulls. They continued to be relentless jerks.

But in spite of everything, I continued to drift. I hadn't even recognized it until Duke pointed it out to me: lost and aimless.

I was in paradise, and yet nothing seemed quite right, ever.

Thanks a lot, Duke.

It wasn't his fault, of course. Just as it wasn't Ma's fault. But you wouldn't have known it from the way we were with each other.

"I've been thinking, Ma," I said over breakfast one morning. It was nearly Labor Day and the end of the season approached. Every summer since I'd started lifeguarding, I felt a bit of a gut twist that let me know things were winding down. Even before I knew what day it was or where we were on the calendar, I awoke just knowing. But my days had a kind of structure then. I knew, like it or not, I'd be going back to school very soon, and that was that and that was acceptable.

This year, I knew no such thing. That was not at all that, and I had no clear idea what was around that Labor Day corner.

Except, there was a that that could be that. It had been creeping up on me and getting into me. Maybe, once again, Duke knew what he was talking about.

"Of course you've been thinking," Ma said. "That's what you do, Fergus. Whenever you're home, you spend all your time thinking. Goodness knows you don't spend it talking."

"Maybe it's conversations like this one that discourage me from trying to have more of them, Mother."

There it was. Why did it have to be like this? I couldn't answer for Ma's side of things, but as for me, I simply couldn't help myself.

She deserved better. But I was becoming convinced that I couldn't produce *better*. Maybe better would mean *alone*. Maybe what she deserved was to have the place to herself.

"Okay, so what I have been thinking is that I might join the service."

If an anvil had dropped from the ceiling and bounced off her head like in a Bugs Bunny cartoon, Ma would have made something like the face she made at this moment. As she clamped down on her toast and froze there, I could just about see a halo of stars spinning around her head.

Because she was a woman of unfailing manners, she completed her task of biting and then slowly chewing her bit of toast before responding.

"Might join . . . what?" she said with unsettling calm.

"The service?" I said.

I put that question mark at the end of my response out of matching manners. Since I had turned eighteen in July, I didn't need permission to do what I wanted to.

However, I still felt I needed *her* permission.

"That would be the *service* in which your father died."

I knew this wouldn't be easy. I just didn't know in exactly what way. I had a pretty good idea now.

"No, Ma. Not that service. One of the other ones."

Sarcasm was not a normal part of my mother's arsenal. So when she unleashed it, it was noticeable.

"Oh joy," she said. Then she commenced crying.

"Nope," I said, pushing my chair back and getting up from the table. "Cannot handle this, Ma. I'm sorry."

It was about an hour early, but I walked straight for the front door. "I'll talk to you later. It'll all be fine. Okay?"

She didn't answer, so I did it myself. "Okay!"

I got in my truck with nothing more than my whistle, my little miniature board that they issue to all the guards, and the brown-bag lunch Ma had made me. I didn't have to look in the bag to know that inside was probably one tuna salad sandwich, one egg salad sandwich, an orange, a sliced beefsteak tomato, and four homemade oatmeal raisin cookies. I could tell from the heft of the package and past experience what the contents were.

I gently placed the bag on my rescue board like a meal tray, set the board on the seat beside me, and tore away from the house before I started bawling myself.

It was a rare overcast day. It didn't feel like rain but didn't feel like sun, either. The beach would be quiet, because at this time of year families preferred bright and constant sunshine. The surf, too, was flat, which meant the beach bum contingent would be small.

Good.

There was one other person on the beach. There was no reason for him to be out there so early, but I wasn't surprised when I found him there.

"You won't be able to surf very fast on that little thing," Duke said, gesturing at the lifeguard board with its two little cutout handles for gripping. "Frankly, I don't even see how it'll support you. Especially with the extra weight you've put on."

I was five foot ten, one hundred thirty pounds. There was no ordinary weight, never mind extra weight. Extra weight would have been more than welcome. Sometimes Duke just said whatever he felt like.

I figured I would give it a shot.

"The Marines are technically part of the Navy, right?" I asked.

Confronted with another conversational version of himself, Duke seemed perplexed. Then pleased.

"Technically, yes," he said, "in much the same way Earth is part of the Milky Way."

"Okay," I said, more seriously. "I've been thinking about the things you were saying."

"Really?" he said, putting on a convincingly concerned expression. "Even I wouldn't recommend that."

"Knock it off for a minute, Duke."

Clearly he could see that I meant business.

"I'm thinking maybe I do want to join up. To the Marines."

It was Duke's turn, for once, to get deadly serious. His face sunk and darkened at once. "You don't want to do that, Fergus," he said.

"What?" I asked, incredulous. "You have been selling me on it all summer. Now you don't want me to follow your advice?"

"My advice was never to join the Marines," he said in a loud whisper, as if we weren't the only two people on a fairly vast beach. He looked right then left over each of his shoulders. "I told you, you belong in the Navy. Or maybe the Coast Guard. But not the Marines, okay?"

"What's the problem?" I asked, feeling thrown a little sideways by his unusual intensity. "I thought you would be pleased."

"The problem, my friend, is that the Marines are not great guys. At least as I've come to know them. I don't think you'd be happy with them."

"Ah, who cares about them?" I said, still agitated about the bust-up with my mother. And the fact that I had gotten this very ball rolling with her. The same ball this guy had first gotten rolling with me. "We could hang around, surfing and hiking and living at Camp Pendleton, just like you talked about. Whenever we aren't off seeing the world, living the easy life and getting paid for it. Like you said."

"Yeah, well, I say lots of things, Fergus. Thing is, you learn more as you move along in this life. And sometimes you learn more than you would like to. And also, coming to California was okay for me, because I got away *to* California. You need to get away *from* California. Just like I needed to get away *from* Hawaii."

I started shaking my head in amazement, as any sensible person would. "Indeed. Then there is that craziness. How can anybody take serious advice from a guy who ran away from Hawaii?"

Duke shook his head a lot more definitively.

"Y'know, Fergus," he said sadly, "most people in the world would say that exact same thing about Southern California. But do you really not get what I mean, about getting away from it?"

I was about to contradict that. Whatever he said, really. I thought for two seconds, maximum three, my finger pointed in his direction.

But he had done it again. He had known *again*.

"I still want to think about it," I said.

"You think about it." Then he got up and started walking away.

"Aren't you staying?" I asked.

"No," he said. "Why would anybody want to waste a day at the beach in this weather?"

"Why did you come to the beach, then?" I asked.

"Same reason I usually come," he said. "To see you. I've done that now. Bye."

"Same time tomorrow?" I called as he strode purposefully away from me.

"It's a date," he called without looking back.

CHAPTER THREE

Dress Blues

Turned out to be a long, lonely day on the beach, though at least I was getting paid for it.

I thought I liked long, lonely days.

Maybe I didn't. At least not anymore.

I guarded lives that, for the most part, weren't there. Two surfers came and went and never presented any lifesaving challenges. I went for a swim to keep myself sharp. I had my lunch, which was a fine lunch and nearly made me weep with its fineness. Then I took an awfully long time digesting it, hoping that the beach remained deserted. If I had to save anybody after eating, the best I'd manage would be sinking to the bottom of the ocean with an oatmeal-raisin grin.

Finally the day ended, and the evening began. I went to my truck. I drove it home. I arrived to yet another lovely meal, lovingly prepared by the lovely woman who sat across from me. It was roast chicken, new potatoes in butter with salt and pepper, and fresh green beans that my home state produced like crazy.

That may sound like a bland and boring dinner, but that couldn't possibly be more wrong. I was going to miss such dinners, as well as the companionship of the silent chef.

And for the third time this day it was an almighty effort not to dissolve in tears.

"Thank you," I said, rasping. "That was wonderful."

"Thank you," she rasped back at me.

The two of us went our separate ways, calling it a night foolishly early. I sat in my bed, reading *Billy Budd* for probably the fifth time but really preoccupied with listening to my mother ghost around the house at the same time. The previous four readings of the book were possibly undone by the same distraction. She finally settled, and the floorboards ceased creaking.

Which was when the gentle sobbing started, in her room down the hall. It was a very similar sound to the creaking, because it was its own creaking.

I fell asleep to that.

I woke as soon as the sun did. I didn't wait for the usual breakfast rituals. As fast as I could manage, I got myself up and down, down and out, without so much as a mousy squeak. I slid through the door, away from the house, toward the truck and into it. She may have heard the engine start up, but by then it was too late.

I had spared us both.

Duke wasn't there when I arrived on the beach. At least, I couldn't see him.

Strangely, though, there were a bunch of Duke look-alikes. Probably a dozen of them, mostly spread across the sand, looking busy and bothered, the way folks do when there's someone lost out there in the water. Three or four of the guys were in the shallows, up to their knees or thighs, gazing up and down the horizon.

As a lifeguard, I knew this action. I'd participated in it a number of times when somebody was unaccounted for, and the family or friends were crazy worried, needing me to find them. I ran down the beach toward the water's edge, yelling out, "What? What's going on, guys?"

They turned as a bunch, toward me, a little frantic.

"Out there! Out! Way out there!" everybody seemed to say all at once, gesturing unhelpfully toward the deep blue sea.

The guys in the shallow water did much the same

thing, pointing the way a third-base coach waves a runner desperately in toward home.

"He's out there, out there, out *there*" was all I could hear, multiplied times a thousand and bounced off every wave and every cliff face before I dove into the water.

I couldn't have said how long I was down there, searching beneath the waves. I'd left my lifesaving board floating on the surface as I searched the depths, desperate and crazed, seeking whoever needed me.

When I finally rose to the surface, I swung toward shore, looking for orientation, looking for help. What I found was a bunch of able-bodied nobodies, fleeing the scene.

"Hey!" I screamed pointlessly. "Heyyy!" I screamed harder once I realized the pointlessness.

I dove again. If I was ever going to break the record for free-diving, this was going to be the time I broke it. And I was going to break it searching for this person.

I knew. I already knew. And I was sickened by what I knew.

If I were honest, I'd say it took me three minutes and a bit of swimming underwater before I saw him. But I could have done much more. I never would have surfaced again until I found him, no matter the cost, and that is the truth.

But I saw him.

He was caught halfway through one of those tunnel rock formations that were a cinch for me or an eel to slither through. Maybe he never would have tried if he hadn't seen me get through it. He was wearing his bathing suit, but on top he had his formal Marine uniform: shirt, tie, and jacket. Dress blues, as they call them.

"Duke!" I garbled, screamed, shrieked, cried underwater.

I swam like a mad fish until I got to him, pulled and shook him the way a shark does with a seal it's devouring. Though my purpose was entirely the opposite. His legs tore up as I yanked him out of the rocks. Blood billowed.

I swam like a creature that had never seen land before, from the time we broke the surface until the time we beached. I must have left a dreadnought's wake behind me.

Once onto packed sand, I started the saving-of-human-life part I had been taught.

I tore open the jacket and tie and gave Duke the most intense chest compressions any rib cage could endure, even *his* steel bars. I did it too quick and too hard. Then

I dropped on him to give him mouth-to-mouth resuscitation.

He repaid me by regurgitating half the ocean into my mouth. I turned to the side, so as not to return the favor when the dead soup ran back out of me. Then I got to work again, compressing his chest, pumping everything out of my friend, listening, leaning into him once more. Breathing his life, my life, into his lungs.

I did this for ten excruciatingly long minutes. Maybe longer.

Until it was beyond clear. His lungs were not cooperating with us.

Finally. Finally, I collapsed on top of him, on top of the uniform they were going to have to dry out to bury him in.

I joined Duke in giving up.

CHAPTER FOUR

Small Fish, Big Pond

I'd happily let him puke in my mouth again.

If only it meant that at the end of it, I'd still have my friend.

But I don't. Because this is the real world.

Odd, the way things turn out sometimes. Duke was in the Marines. But he wanted me to join the Navy. Yet I wanted to become a Marine, like him. And then he died, with a bunch of US (Useless Slug) Marines right there, watching it happen.

I could never join that Marine Corps.

So it was as much a tribute to Duke as anything else when I didn't sign up for his Marine Corps. Instead, I joined the Navy like he'd told me to.

I decided I wanted for me what he wanted for me. To achieve a good life, test myself, use my natural and acquired skills, and see the world while it was largely at peace.

This journey began with a trip that was no trip at

all, really. One of the major aims and most compelling points of Duke's advice to me was that I was going to see the world. And just like his quest to leave behind the legendary and desirable Hawaii had to do with a young man's need to get away from home at a certain point, mine was going to be to leave the relative comfort of Southern California to the tourists and beach bums.

So where did the Navy send me right out of the chute?

The Naval Training Center at San Diego. Less than sixty miles from my front door.

So much for freedom and independence. My mother could bring me my lunch.

Well, no, she could not.

Because in truth, *everything* was moving, and I knew it from the start. At boot camp in San Diego, I could feel the air changing. I was tested and taught the limits of my abilities. I learned to march, to follow orders no matter how stupid, to polish my shoes until I could clearly see the shoe-polishing idiot grimacing back at me from the sheen. I learned how to handle a rifle and to march with that rifle held high over my head for an hour. I learned more about the water than I ever dreamed of—and I'd spent my whole life dreaming about it.

I learned how to function as part of a team, whether I liked it or not.

I did not like it, just for the record. But I understood it, and that was progress.

I learned everything about naval-vessel identification, ordinance handling, ropes, and general seamanship, all of which was new and exciting in ways I hadn't expected. I also learned I was no slouch with a potato peeler.

When basic was over, it was time for recruits to move on, move up, and move out into that wider world we'd been promised. Some of us would be going straight into service aboard ships or at various naval installations around the world. Others would be moving on to advanced training, based on what kind of skills and aptitude we showed, and how we scored in the multitude of tests the Navy was always putting us through.

I shouldn't have been surprised when it was decided I'd be sent to the training program at the Naval Amphibious Base in Coronado, California.

It was directly across the bay from where I already was. I could have literally swum there on my own.

And my mother still could have been there to greet me with a couple sandwiches and a stack of cookies.

But the truth was, I was thrilled to be going. Despite the fact that I'd barely left Orange County, four months after honoring my deceased pal's wishes for me to see the world, I knew I was on my way.

When I got to Coronado, perhaps the biggest surprise of all was that I found guys like me. Water rats, naturally, but also real enthusiasts. This meant that while our work was still *work*, pretty much everybody seemed to have a ball carrying it out.

Since the bulk of amphibious naval work involved slick and secretive reconnaissance and assault missions, we got to spend a lot of our training time in Coronado practicing getting in and out of hostile coastal situations. I was part of a group known as Underwater Demolition Team Three—and who in his right mind wouldn't love to be part of a name like that? It was like all the fun things in life bundled up together. The team itself was actually a rather sprawling thing. It might have had up to around one hundred members, all spread out among the various waterworks operations going on at the base and beyond. But I only saw large numbers when we were all brought together for drills and exercises and such.

For practical purposes, I belonged to a team within the team. Lt. Atcheson, an older, experienced guy in his late twenties, was basically our boss. It was obvious that the chain of command had a lot of respect and confidence in Lt. Atcheson, because he was left largely alone to run our training as he sought fit. He also had a certain amount of discretion to select talent when he identified it. Over the course of our months training at Coronado, there would be guys who would come into the team suddenly, guys who would leave again suddenly, and we would get very little explanation as to why.

The common denominator regarding who stayed and who went seemed to come down to what Lt. Atcheson thought of the guy.

He wasn't mean or excessive. Maybe in the real world he would qualify as a tough-nut boss to work for. But in the Navy, we had seen what mean and hard actually looked like. Many, if not most, officer types sneer and scream at the people under them so viciously that I wondered on a regular basis if we'd been infiltrated by enemy personnel. There was just no way that the treatment a new recruit received from his commanding boss could be any worse than what he'd receive if he was captured by the bad guys.

And yes, the logic was that if we do this to you and you can take it, then there's nothing anybody else can do to you that you cannot withstand.

To which I have to say . . . nonsense.

Because I can also say . . . Lt. Atcheson.

I would never say that the lieutenant was a softy, or a fool, or anything other than a smart, educated, experienced leader of men. But he was also a walking, talking, diving example of how you don't have to break down your men in order to get them to respect you in the military. There was never anything he asked us to do that he didn't do right alongside us.

I would also never say that he was what you would call a friend.

Lt. Atcheson knew who he wanted and who he didn't because of how good they'd be at the job, how reliable under pressure, how willing to do *any* crazy thing they were asked in order to achieve a goal they may or may not have understood.

And, most of all, how well they could be relied upon not to get themselves, their comrades, or their "chief benefactor" (aka Lt. Atcheson) killed in the line of duty.

I felt that I could meet those requirements.

That's why he and I got along quite well right from the start.

That was also why, within very short order, I came to have complete confidence in every guy on the team. If Lt. Atcheson decided you were all right, then you were all right with me.

Even if some of the guys weren't even Navy. Turned out that the specialized group I was training with—UDTs—accepted volunteers from all the services: Army, Navy, Coast Guard, Air Force . . . even Marines. As long as you were physically fit and mentally unfit enough to want to spend your time blowing things up underwater, you could join the fun.

And the fun, on many days, was a jumped-up version of what I had been spending my recent summers doing at San Onofre.

"Paddle, paddle, paddle, paddle!" yelled Lt. Atcheson as eight of us did just that, with all our might. We had already been paddling, hard, before he started shouting at us. But we were getting defeated by the waves. Our team of eight had just delivered two other guys onto the beach. The big inflatable boat we were paddling was basically the center of operations for everything an Underwater Demolition Team did. The trip back out past the break line of the surf was about a thousand times more demanding than the trip in, thus the extra bellowing. Not that it had been a piece of cake before. The waves were already having a feisty day, but this was another beast entirely.

On the way in, it was clear that ten guys on a raft

would not just be an enlarged version of a single guy on a board trying to catch a wave.

I found myself shouting more than once that if the rest of them would just bail out, I could surf the boat in myself without any problem. And a few times it looked like I was going to get my wish. The waves succeeded in flipping a couple of the men up in the air and out of the boat, and we nearly capsized twice. I'd been whitewater rafting a few times, and this was the closest I had come to that on the ocean.

Having deposited our two amphibious friends on the beach to simulate an insertion for an interdiction, we had to rush with as little fanfare as possible back beyond the break. There, we'd wait for the signal to retrieve them again.

The surf was angry. It had become one of those days that surfers live for but that make eight guys on an inflatable wish they were infantry.

"Perhaps you men didn't hear me," Lt. Atcheson yelled. A second consecutive breaker broke over us and turned us back toward the beach. "I said, *paddle*! *That way*!" He pointed in the opposite direction, seaward, in case we were confused.

Just before we righted the boat, I caught a glimpse

of the two lucky landlubbers we'd left on the beach, laughing and waving at us before tumbling to the sand in hysterics.

Colavito, who we'd already come to know as having the biggest bravado in the team, shouted back at the lieutenant. "We are paddling! What you think we're doing here, catching butterflies?"

Several guys laughed, which was just as bad an idea as yelling at the boss. I was neither yelling nor laughing, but I still managed to swallow half a lung full of seawater for my troubles.

I was thinking that this was the very reason I never joined any teams. Not that I'd ever been in this particular situation before. But if I had—trying to work as one with a bunch of crazy and strong-willed young guys, all from different services and all with different histories—then this would be the exact reason for my solitary nature.

"Like this," I heard as we fell back again and a wave of foamy white burned my eyes and nostrils.

The speaker was a guy named Sheldon, who was across the raft from me, in the second row behind Atcheson and Colavito. In addition to shouting, Sheldon got my attention by whacking me on the arm with his paddle.

Sheldon was one of the deep blue Navy guys, the kind of guy with gills where his ears should be. Like everybody else, he'd acquired a sea life–related nickname—Shellfish—though he'd already had his when he joined up.

He was probably the first guy other than the lieutenant who I learned to listen closely to. He got almost violent now as he demonstrated what he thought of as the proper method for paddling us out of a whitewash like this one.

After he had paddled *me*, Shellfish went over and attacked his side of the water. I nearly lunged over and grabbed him when I thought he was going overboard, but it turned out to be his method. He forced the top half of his body down on top of the water with each powerful stroke, then came up and did it again. He repeated the action over and over, with the power of a leaping and diving dolphin.

Shellfish paused briefly to look at me and register that I had registered. Then he made a mini-stroke motion, followed by three and then four more until we were in the same rhythm, and then he yelled, "Go!"

And go we did. Next thing I knew, I was down into the water almost to my waist, before pulling back up.

I could see Sheldon moving in perfect sync as we did it again, and again, and again.

I knew we were doing something right when I caught the lieutenant looking back over his shoulder with surprise on his face. Sheldon and I were pumping with such machinelike power and precision, we were thrusting the boat forward even from our second-banana positions. It was a little like a highway automobile pileup, and we were forcing the guys at the front to jam it up a gear.

The waves continued to crash over us, to the point where there was as much Pacific Ocean inside the boat as all around it. Then we felt the pressure as the guys behind us got in the same rhythm. The next wave was a whopper. It would have crashed us all the way back to the beach if we hadn't been laying into it like we were.

Instead, it broke over us like a sweet misty spring breeze. We pounded our way past the break line where surf was old news, then shouted and screamed like we'd successfully escaped Alcatraz.

Even Lt. Atcheson was something like impressed.

"Men," he said, standing tall and turning back to address the lot of us like George Washington crossing the Delaware on that little dinghy, "I think you may be getting the hang of it."

Everybody was huffing hard, competing with the lieutenant's voice and the ocean's *lap-yapp*ing at the sides of our boat. But things were already a lot more settled than they had been on the other side of the break. I knew, broadly, what we were to do now. But since there was no actual mission for the two drop-off guys to complete, I started to wonder as we rode gently up and down the swells for a couple minutes.

Then I needed wonder no more.

"Mr. Frew," the lieutenant said, getting once more to his feet.

"Yes, sir, Lieutenant," I answered.

"Frew," he said, "this is your lucky day. Do you recall, as this *team* of ours was fighting against the powerful surf, trying to keep the boat and ourselves upright against the considerable force of nature in order to carry out our mission . . ."

This was already looking bad.

"Do you recall, Frew, expressing any thoughts as to how the operation might go better if you had your way?"

Rats. Of course I remembered. As did all the snickering sailors around me. I was kind of hoping the lieutenant might not quite remember, though he didn't appear to be the forgetful type.

"Yes, sir, Lieutenant."

"What was it you said again? Something about how you wished you could be taking the boat into the shore and out again against the surf by yourself?"

"I believe it was something like that, sir. But the thing was—"

"Gentlemen!" the lieutenant rudely interrupted, though rudely interrupting was very much his right. "Every man not named Frew will now kindly enter the water!"

With shocking speed and enthusiasm, the remaining men splashed into the sea around us.

"Now," Lt. Atcheson said, pointing along an imaginary line running parallel to the coast, "you all will spread yourselves out along this line, leaving approximately fifty feet between each of you. This will be our pickup line when the boat comes back out to retrieve you. Your job is to get to your position, and then hold it exactly so that the boat can find you with minimum effort. As we will ordinarily be carrying out such operations under cover of night, it is of vital importance that you master the basic art of *finding your spot and holding that spot. Is that crystal clear to each of you?*"

"Yes, sir, Lieutenant!" they yelled as one obedient school of fish-men.

"And, men," he said, pointing out to sea, "should you fail to hold your spots, and the pickup boat cannot locate you, it will be *your* job to swim back out to the ship."

He was pointing to the training vessel that had deposited our boat into the water. About a mile out. "Off you go!"

"Lieutenant," Colavito called before they all took off.

"Yes, Colavito?"

"I'd like to volunteer to go with Frew and retrieve the other men."

"Well," Lt. Atcheson said, "that is very generous of you. But since Frew specifically requested a solo trip, and I decided to grant that request, I am of a mind to leave things as is. But I tell you what . . ."

The lieutenant turned in my direction. "Frew," he said, "when you reach the beach, just collect Dover. Tell Muskie to sit tight there, and Mr. Colavito will be in directly to ferry him back out."

Lt. Atcheson turned to address the boys bobbing in the water once more. "How's that?" he said. "Win-win, right?"

The men resumed swimming out to their assigned spots. I was just about to ask Lt. Atcheson what next, when he, too, dropped into the water. He popped up to the surface again, checking his watch. "Let's see what kind of time you can make, Mr. Frew," he said.

I started paddling madly.

At first, things were going pretty well. When it came to surfing the waves inland, I really did know what I was talking about. Perhaps it was wishful thinking, but it seemed like less trouble negotiating my way into the beach alone than we'd had as a team. It wasn't easy, by any means, but I felt like I was living within the wave, not unlike the way I always did as a board or body surfer. With the team involved, we had a lot more horsepower, but it felt partly like we were doing battle with ourselves. The boat was pushing and pulling until we were like a fat rubber whirlpool working its way to the bottom of the ocean, rather than the outer edge of it.

But that was before we'd coalesced into a dynamic unit, like one organism with one mind and a lot of muscle power.

By the time I beached, and Dover and Muskie ran up to flop themselves into the boat, I was pretty well tuckered out, successful journey or no.

"Uh-uh," I panted, pushing Muskie back out toward

the beach. "You're supposed to wait for the next trip. Lieutenant's orders."

Muskie raised a fist and opened his mouth to complain, out of reflex. But then he looked up at the clear sky, kicked at a bit of smooth sand, and did the sensible thing.

"Okay," he said, and went back to relaxing on the beach.

"So how did I get stuck with you?" Dover asked, as the two of us sat winded and weak in the shallows. The surf had beat us back toward shore three times now. I was so yearning to be surfing this rather than fighting it. "Did I do something wrong?"

"No," I wheezed, "you didn't do anything. It was me. I made the mistake of saying that I could handle the raft for both drop-off and pickup better by myself than the whole crew could."

"Whooo-hoo-hoo," Dover whistled in response. Whistling was Dover's natural response to just about everything. He was something like a professional whistler, and could make himself sound like a bugle or a harmonica or so much like a whale that I sometimes had to check the horizon to see if he'd called any in. Most of the time as he whistled through his work, it made the days way more pleasant just to hear it. Right now, it was causing me extra embarrassment.

"Whooo-hoo-hoo," he whistled again, after taking a few more seconds to think about it.

"All right, all right," I said. The embarrassment caused me to burst into a ferocious paddling attack. But all that did was force the boat into a pathetic little spin. That's what happens when one side of a boat gets paddled while the other one gets whistled.

"Okay," he said, joining me and getting us oriented into the waves once more. The surf had calmed, but only slightly. We caught an eight-footer straight in the face, but we had saved up enough strength to burst through it.

"There we go, boy," I said, as the two of us increased power, windmilling our paddles in anticipation of the next one.

"That's about the worst kind of thing you can say around here, you know that," Dover said, just as the next wave broke over us.

"I can think of worse," I said.

"I wouldn't if I were you. Unless you would like to disappear from the team. If Lt. Atcheson gets a whiff that you aren't all-for-one-one-for-all, then you'll be gone before you can even show him what you can do. That's as close as we get around here to a golden rule."

We blasted through another wave, then one more, the two of us generating considerable power—seahorse power—by pumping along in perfect unison, perfect symmetry.

And just like that, we were through, and we were sailing. The ocean had calmed to a gentle roll and the sun shone on us like we'd burst through a cloud rather than a wave break.

As we headed toward the line of bobbing boys in the water, I got to paddle along to Dover's whistling of "I'm looking over a four-leaf clover that I overlooked before . . ."

CHAPTER FIVE

Another Graduation

We spent a large and ever-growing proportion of our time in the training pool. We worked on lifesaving and first aid, which I already knew so well I was practically teaching it to the other guys. We practiced handling weapons and explosives above and below the surface. We had all kinds of races and competitions against the clock and against one another.

More than anything, we swam, swam, swam.

Something that *was* entirely new to me was the underwater breathing apparatus. It was called LARU, which stood for Lambertsen Amphibious Respiratory Unit. It was named after the guy who thought it up in the 1940s. It involved three tanks of compressed air strapped on to a diver's back and connected to his mouth by a hose and mouthpiece, fitted below the face mask. One highly useful element to it was a sort of release valve that was attached to the diver's chest. This valve allowed for the release of expelled air without producing that whole crazy-bubbles effect that previous gear produced. Those bubbles were not only embarrassing, but when expelled by a demolition diver sneaking in or out of an enemy harbor, they'd very likely get him identified and killed.

In short, LARU was a brilliant and useful piece of equipment. All the guys in our group fell in love with it. LARU sessions in the training pool were like recess in a primary school playground for the likes of us.

But I hated it.

"Lieutenant," I called out, pulling myself up onto the side of the pool when I saw him.

"Yes, Mr. Frew," he said, walking over all genial and helpful like the village postman or something. He was generally like that, as long as you didn't upset him.

"I will not be needing that," I said politely, carefully.

"Oh, you won't, won't you?"

Having been down this particular slippery slipway with the lieutenant before, I scrambled casually backward.

"What I mean is, Lieutenant," I said, "I will of course obey any command I receive, in any situation that presents itself. But given my druthers, I'd just prefer to use my natural ability at swimming and holding my breath whenever possible."

It was, in a way, kind of him to cover his mouth with his hand as he shielded me from a rather unprofessional laugh.

When the moment had passed, he sought to enlighten me a bit. "One might say, Frew, that a man who has voluntarily joined the United States Navy, and further joined a specialist, demanding, dangerous outfit like ours, might not consider it one of his life's priorities to be given his *druthers*."

I sunk a bit lower but kept looking up at him.

"That is a fair point indeed, sir. I just wanted to point out that whenever possible, I feel like I'll be of greater use to our efforts if I'm allowed to free-dive. I am really quite good at it. I can stay submerged for—"

"I know all about it," he said. Then he laughed again as he spun away from me. "That would be the reason the men refer to you as Frogus."

"What?" I said, turning away from him and toward my pals frolicking in the water. "Who's been calling me Frogus?"

All I could do was pretend to be outraged. In reality, I loved it.

And the nickname made me feel extra proud when the next week, our final training week, came around. So far we'd done our work in the pool and the lovely warm waters of San Diego Bay, requiring nothing more to cover us than swimming trunks and whatever gear we were hauling.

But rumor had it there were hotspots around the globe that were not so hot at all. Certainly colder than what we'd known so far.

There was something very official feeling in the moment one afternoon when Lt. Atcheson and his top assistant, Boatswain's Mate (BM3) Ravens, gathered us on the deck of the training ship. They lined us up like a sort of graduation ceremony and presented each of us with our rubber dry suits.

This was when we finally and fully appreciated why UDT divers were known as Frogmen. We looked like long strung-up frogs in these outfits.

It took practically half the afternoon and a great deal of teamwork, but eventually we got the whole unit into dry suits and down the ropes onto the waiting boat below. This vessel was bigger than what we'd trained on, a Landing Craft, Personnel (Ramped), an LCP(R), which was one of the legendary boats that delivered troops to beaches all over the world in the war. It was popularly known as a Higgins boat. Just being aboard the vessel, manned by regular Navy crew members, was a whole new level of importance I hadn't experienced before. Looking around me at all the goofy grins as we steamed into harbor, I knew I wasn't alone in that feeling.

We spent virtually all of that final training week in and out of amphibious boats, in and out of Frogman dry suits. They were surprisingly snug and comfortable, and not overly warm as long as the weather cooperated. Luckily we dealt with a lot of uncharacteristically cool and wet weather for the area. Usually I did most of my practice recon and charge-setting duties with just my dry suit and my mask on, and that was fine. A few times, though, the lieutenant insisted I dive out in the deeper waters with the breathing gear. We all needed to be prepared for everything.

And that turned out to be a very good thing. Being ready for anything.

On the last day of training, as we prepared for our passing out ceremony (meaning out into the world, rather than out of consciousness), Lt. Atcheson called a bunch of us into his office.

In addition to himself and BM3 Ravens, it was Colavito, Dover, Sheldon, and me.

Or more informally: Baccala (Italian for codfish), Sole (Dover sole being a delicious delicacy, apparently), Shellfish, and Frogus. Ravens's nickname was Dogfish, as he was less than average in the handsomeness department. We also had an above-average handsome teammate named Chamberlain, whose nickname was Chum. Not that he was particularly friendly—he wasn't, to anybody but his own rugged reflection in the mirror—but because chum is the fish bits you throw into the water to attract other fish. Chum was not otherwise very useful.

"This is a big day, men," Lt. Atcheson said. He paced around behind his desk while the rest of us huddled in front of it. It was all kinds of cramped, but Navy men get used to that. "Today marks the day when you move up from being trainees to being highly skilled, respected, and yes, feared members of the country's most elite Special Forces operations. There are quite a few of you stepping across that line later, but I wanted to take a moment to speak to a select group of you, because this is important."

This was why I tended to skip graduation days.

"You men are not just trained, skilled, and hardened, you are also part of a special *team*."

I may have imagined it, but I felt sure he singled me out with a stare on that last word.

"As individuals, there's nobody like you. You volunteered for naval duty and then again for specialist UDT duty. You are all, in a sense, rogues."

Every one of us loved that. We really were still kids, at the end of the day.

"But that's not enough. As you all already know." His seriousness increased with every word, as he pointed along the line at each of us individually. "Because if you're nothing more than a collection of daring, talented adventurers, then you will almost certainly die as a result. What makes you all truly special is that you are a *team* of rogues, a *collective* of rogues. That, men, is what will make this group of ours something unstoppable, something unlike any fighting force ever seen anywhere."

The whole room erupted to that, howling and slapping backs, elbowing and shoving until we were bouncing off the walls and tumbling over the desk.

"All right, that's enough!" Lt. Atcheson bellowed. And when we finally settled, he resumed in a more measured voice.

"So, tomorrow, men," he said, "our unit is to be deployed. We are being sent as a team to the beaches of Japan."

There was more shouting and howling then, but of a much more mature kind. At least I thought so.

"And I hope you don't mind," the lieutenant said casually as he settled finally into his desk chair, "but we'll be required to endure a one-week stopover in Hawaii."

I didn't even participate in this round of celebrating. In fact, I was so excited I nearly passed out—this time, the loss-of-consciousness kind.

In addition to failing to attend my high school graduation, thus depriving my long-suffering mother of what are supposed to be defining emotional pinpoints on the child-raising map, I likewise failed to make even a passing fuss over my graduation from boot camp. Despite the fact that my family home was possibly the closest of any other boot's, and the fact that my mother would have crawled commando-style all the way to the ceremony, and the fact that I surely owed her something, I didn't alert her when the time came.

What was wrong with me?

Something kicked in with this one, though. Maybe it had to do with the time spent under Lt. Atcheson, and the graceful way he had with getting meaningful lessons across. Maybe it was the time spent with the guys themselves, the way circumstances and personalities conspired to meld us together in ways I never would have predicted, much less sought.

Maybe it was another thing I never saw coming, though I probably should have.

I was now, finally, leaving home.

I'd already left it, of course. Left it in stages when I chose my surfboard over my house. Left it again when I joined the Navy. Left it again when I crossed the bay and volunteered for the UDT.

But this was a far bigger leap. I was leaving home, leaving my ma, leaving my history. Physically and otherwise, I was never really gone before this.

After graduating from amphibious training, I was overwhelmed with the need to go see my ma.

I took a bus along the short but pleasant route between Coronado and San Clemente. I wore my uniform, the famous Navy whites with the funny dog bowl hat and everything. I knocked on the door, unannounced but all polite-like.

When she answered, Ma made precisely the same sort of gasp I make prior to diving under the water.

She didn't do more than that. Not at first. With her hand over her mouth, she sized me up and down. And up. And down. I resigned myself to standing there for as long as this process was going to take.

And then I decided it was taking too long.

"Are you going to let me in, ma'am?"

She looked surprised again, like she hadn't considered this. Then she pulled me inside, forcefully enough to make me stumble and laugh out loud.

She sat me at the kitchen table, and I let her. Then she started fussing with foodstuffs, even though I asked her not to. In a few minutes, a very few minutes, an unfeasibly few minutes, I had a chicken salad sandwich, a bowl of exquisite homemade potato salad, and a plate of chocolate chip cookies in front of me. It was as if she'd been prepared for this eventuality—this very day.

Despite not being hungry, I knew better than to not eat. I didn't want to get her started.

She got started anyway.

"You are so skinny," she said, pointing vaguely in the direction of my abdomen.

"It's the uniform, Ma. Everybody looks like this. Think about it, have you ever seen a fat sailor?"

"I don't recall ever seeing a sailor at all," she said seriously. "I must have, but I never took any notice until just now. It only matters to me now because of you."

Not sure how I had missed this for so long. What a love she was. Guess I was too busy being a jerk.

She was being a good sport. But it had to be hard for her. Not only was her experience with Navy uniforms limited, it would be the same with uniforms of all kinds. It primarily came down to seeing my dad in his gear. That would have been how he looked the last time she saw him. She sent him off in that uniform and then he was dead.

And while the Army's uniforms were quite low-key compared to the dress-up box the Navy played out of, you'd have to believe it all looked the same to her.

The welling up of her eyes as I made my way through my lunch indicated this was the case. It certainly wasn't her pride in my ability to chew each bite thirty-two times.

"Ma," I finally said.

"Shush," she finally answered.

We technically spoke on the phone once a week. But we were both appalling phone conversationalists at the best of times. So one might think we had a lot of catching up to do here. One might be disappointed, however.

Instead, she got up and left me at the table to finish my cookies on my own. She went to her room and fussed around in there for a while, before coming back out and taking her seat across from me again. She presented a gift-wrapped cube roughly big enough to contain my fist. She slid it across the table, while at the same time deftly collecting my lunch plates. As if clearing the table was her actual agenda.

"Ah, Ma," I said, unaware of the box's contents, but still.

"I can give you a small something," she said while trucking my debris to the sink. "Can I not give you a small something?"

"What's the reason?" I said, fighting what shouldn't have been fought. Because I was the world's most pointlessly awkward son. "What's the occasion?"

I never gave her enough credit. She knew things. She always knew things. And I never gave her the credit.

"It's a graduation present," she said matter-of-factly. "It's all the graduation presents."

Just a modest little package. But there, just like that, it got so huge right before my eyes. First, I simply stared at it, as if it could do me harm. Funny behavior for a supposed explosives expert. I was trained for those other kind of explosions, though. I had nothing to prepare me for what might be popping out of this.

But eventually, you just have to go at it, don't you?

I went at it, didn't I?

I peeled away the wrapping, shredding it to bits once I started. The paper flew up and sideways and down before settling all over the floor. Put me to mind of the confetti parades in New York when we won the war. The war we won when we lost my dad.

"Ah," I said when I opened up the box. "Ah," I repeated, followed by, "Ah, Ma."

"You've wanted it for a long time, Fergus, yes?"

For several seconds, I struggled to speak.

"Yes."

It was a rugged and indestructible diver's watch. You could swim to the bottom of the ocean with it, the surf could beat you on the rocks like a grizzly bear mangling a salmon, and this watch would forge ahead, telling the time to within a hundredth of a second. This was the watch every watch aspired to be. If Kirk Douglas were a watch, this was the watch he would be.

"Ma," I said. "Ma?"

"Ha," she said. "I finally got you speechless."

It probably cost half of my father's life insurance for her to buy the thing. And she had probably been hanging on to it since the day I skipped my high school graduation.

Ah, Ma.

"Ah, Ma," I said. I rose from my seat, walked around the table, and hugged her, like the son she never had.

"Oh, don't be such a mush," she said through sniffles.

"I should have been better, Ma. I know that. I should have cared more. I should have tried."

"Shush," she said again. Shush being her all-purpose conversation ender. "You're going now," she said.

Again, she knew. She knew I was shoving off, probably before I did. Probably before Atcheson did. I was stupid to think I could tell her stuff, and withhold stuff.

I nodded from beneath my stupid hat.

"Where?" she asked.

"Japan. Via Hawaii, though."

She feigned pleasure. "You've always wanted to go. Bravo, son. Do some mighty surfing while you're there, right?"

"I will, Ma," I said, acting as if the difficult parts of this were now over.

She wouldn't have that, though. She seized my face in her strong, knowing hands.

"I want to see you again, son. I need to see you. I've done my part. You cannot be your own island out there anymore. You need a team. Trust somebody. You're going to need to learn to trust. Please, *please*, trust."

Her need for this was so strong, I almost collapsed in front of her.

"I have a good team," I said.

With a depth of sadness I had never seen before, not even from her, she said, "I don't believe you."

I was badly losing a battle I had never seen coming. And like all the big battles, I had no chance of winning this one on my own.

"Ma," I said urgently, "I have to go."

"What?" she said. "But, Fergus, you just got here."

She would have to say that. It's in the moms' play-book, probably. I could have stayed twelve hours and she would still say that I just got there.

"No, no," I said, taking both of her hands in mine. I was so unfamiliar with those hardworking hands. Their roughness surprised me. I found myself staring at them. "I'm coming right back. Trust me. Stay at the front window. Sit in the window seat. I'm going to show you something."

For whatever reason, I felt the need to lead her from the kitchen to the front room and right down into the window seat. And for her own reasons, she let me.

"You'll stay right there, then," I said.

"I will," she said.

I grabbed the keys to my truck, hanging right there on the hook by the front door where I had left them months ago.

What was I going to do with that truck? I didn't want to think about it.

"Sit right there," I said, rushing out the front door and into my waiting, loyal vehicle.

I went straight to the mess hall. There I found all my guys eating together, hanging around together, though this wasn't required in their free time.

"Guys," I said dramatically, "I need you. All of you."

Every single one of them reacted to my urgency and jumped up out of their seats.

"What? What is it, Froggy? What do you need? What's wrong? What's happening?"

In an instant, they made me wonder why I never saw the value of good friends before.

"I need you to meet my mom!" I said with the same

kind of urgency that Lassie the dog would employ to alert humans to trouble down at the old mill.

"Yeeaahh!" was the gist of what I heard out of my comrades.

It was with Lassie's same blessed canine enthusiasm that all my teammates bounded along with me to pile into the rusty Plymouth pickup.

They also had the good sense to love the old thing as much as I did. I could hear the bunch of them rumbling and bumbling around in the bed, yipping and playing around like a litter of pups. Up front, crammed into the cab with me, were Colavito and Dover.

"Not a bad tin can you got here, Frog," Colavito said.

"Bit rough around the edges," Dover said, "but it sure has character."

"Aw, now I like it less," Colavito said. "People only say a thing has character when it obviously has nothing going for it at all."

"Hit a nerve there, did I, Baccala?" Dover said. "Pretty sure I heard the lieutenant talking about your *sparkling* character just this morning."

"Har-har," Colavito answered. "For your information, nobody has ever said that to me in my life."

This of course made Dover laugh uncontrollably.

Much as I was enjoying the festivities, we'd be home

shortly, and I needed to be sure these guys were in presentable form.

"All right," I said, mock-sternly, "any more of this carrying on and I'll turn this truck right around and take you kids back to the base."

"No, please, no, Dad!" Dover said.

"Yeah," Colavito added, "we'll be good. We promise."

"That's better," I said.

I hit a pothole, rattling the Plymoth's bones, exposing her old stiffness and tossing around the guys in back like a big salad. I got howls of protest from back there, which made even a pothole seem worthwhile.

"Anyway," I said, "it is a great vehicle for a surfer."

"You're a surfer?" Colavito asked in a forced high-pitched voice. "I didn't know that. I can't stand surfers."

"Have to agree with Codfish on this one, Frogus. I kinda can't stand 'em, either. Perhaps you should let us out here."

"Perhaps I should!" I snapped. Then I laughed along with them. "Actually, I don't much like them, myself." We turned the corner up my street. "Now, please," I said, "can you guys behave yourselves?" I was looking up at my mother in the front window seat, right where I had left her.

"I don't think we can make any promises, Frog," Dover answered. "Baccala, you think we can make any promises?"

"I don't think we can, Sole."

"Great," I said, pulling on the emergency break and cutting the engine. "That's just swell, guys, thanks."

It cheered me up to see the genuinely astonished look on my mother's face. The number of guys piling out of my truck was probably greater than the number of friends I had had over to the house my entire life.

She got to the door before we did, threw it open, and stood there to greet us with an impossible grin that would make clown makeup look subtle.

"Ma," I said, already embarrassed, "could you calm yourself a little? The guys are going to think I'm sad and friendless."

"Well, you are sad and friendless," she said, waving us all in with immediacy.

"So," I said, shaking my head as I headed toward the kitchen, "it's going to be like this, is it?"

But I couldn't begrudge her the smile. I'd never seen her as happy as this little thing was making her.

Once gathered in the kitchen, introductions were in order.

"Ma, this guy here is David Dover the Diver. That guy there is Baccala, the handsome one is Dogfish, the guy with the eggplant-shaped head is Squid. Then you've got Clay the Crayfish, Sheldon the Shellfish. Then that last guy is Muskie, who doesn't get a nickname because he already sounds like a sea creature.

"Guys," I said, "this is my ma."

"Hey, Ma!" every one of them called out. Or words to that effect.

It had seemed before like she was already prepared to feed me, even though there was no reason to be prepared. But this was even more impressive. Within minutes, Ma produced cold cuts, ham, and liverwurst, plus Swiss cheese and a big crusty loaf of bread that she made Baccala cut with the serrated knife. There was a bowl of potato salad and a bunch of red-to-bursting huge tomatoes, and of course a whole mess of home-made cookies.

I was instructed to get out plates and napkins and whatnot for this bunch of seagoing savages. When I did, they threw themselves on the bounty like they'd been shipwrecked without proper provisions for months.

They had all just eaten, too.

Ma was beyond heaven. Whatever the place that looks down on heaven, that was where she was now.

"Ma," I said quietly to her while the guys entertained her with their seagull-like approach to food. "Why would you have all this food here when it's just you? I mean, even when I lived here I never brought a bunch like this home with me. What gives?"

She just watched them, so intently that I wasn't sure she'd heard me.

"Ma, how come—"

"You just never know, do you?" she said, turning her head to look me deep in the eyes.

And it was true. You just never know lots of stuff. Maybe you never know anything at all. I definitely never would have known any of this was possible. For sure not that the guys would spend nearly two hours at my mother's table, goofing around and acting like children, charming her into submission . . . and reassuring her.

Who knew? Who knew this would have been possible? I dreamed up this mini mission for exactly this purpose, so that my ma could meet my guys and my guys could make her feel better about my prospects. Show her that my prospects looked better than Dad's.

The best laid plans of frogs and men can come good once in a while, I guess.

And to be fair, my dad did have a war to fight. We didn't.

CHAPTER SIX

Anchors Aweigh

We left San Diego Harbor the second week of June 1950. We were a ten-man contingent carved out of the larger Underwater Demolition Team Three and were traveling along as guests on a destroyer. UDTs basically never had homes of their own, and so were always hopping rides with vessels that were going where we needed to go. Appropriate that we were always hopping, homeless bunch of frogs that we were.

The destroyer rendezvoused with a task force that included four other destroyers, four oilers, and two cruisers. None of us had any idea why so many vessels were shipping out at once, but I don't think any of us cared much, either. We were starting on the big adventure, to see the world.

And we were going to surf the promised land of surfing—or at least I was. Though that probably should have been the promised *waters* of surfing.

It took five long days of sailing to get there, and I spent a good bit of it throwing up alongside some of my mates. We had all spent time aboard boats, of course, but we hadn't spent time crossing the vast and mighty Pacific. Nor were we aware of just how top-heavy the deceptively beautiful and sleek US Navy destroyers were.

The thing rocked and rolled basically every hour of those five days. Not only were we a nauseated bunch of frogs, we were also periodically skittled around the ship like balls in a pachinko machine.

Added to that, the actual crew of the ship was put through surprisingly strenuous training the whole way. Because so much of the Navy's personnel were dismissed at the end of the war, there were loads of new guys on the job these days. They needed all the training they could get. And these destroyers, bless their lethal guts, were rampant with opportunities for practicing with live and lively firepower.

The ship carried six five-inch, 38-caliber dual-purpose guns in dual mounts, sixteen 40-mm antiaircraft guns in four quad mounts, two batteries that fired twenty "hedgehog" antisubmarine mortars each, and five 21-inch torpedo tubes.

For much of the time, it sounded like they were all being tested at once.

But all was forgiven when we pulled into port at Pearl Harbor. We'd seen about a million photographs of the place, so it was like we had all been there before.

Still, that didn't help with the sadness that came over me like a tidal wave as we cruised in slowly along the long slipway and everyone saluted the entire way.

Once we settled in, we were welcomed into the base. I was looking forward to some chow and a good night's sleep without the turmoil of the open sea.

I didn't think the weather could get any better than Southern California, but there was something about this place that added a sweet extra. The air itself tasted different: saltier, greener somehow, and certainly wetter. It was heavy on the tongue, and the skies at sunset were streaky and layered in so many reds, oranges, and pinks that I wondered for a few minutes whether my brain was making it all up.

So that first evening was quietly blissful. Our plan had been to go sightseeing, as a full complement of frogs. But one by one, the guys all begged off. The truth was, I was so legless with fatigue that nothing sounded as thrilling to me as some peaceful sleep.

Nothing, that was, except the thought of tomorrow's trip to Maui.

It was as deep a sleep as I could ever remember having. Ten hours after hitting the rack—the benefits of being mere passengers rather than crew—we were awakened to all sorts of commotion all over the ship.

The *moving* ship.

"What's happening, Lieutenant?" I asked, scrambling to catch up with the guys who were already gathered around him.

"We are shipping out, men," he said flatly.

"We shipped out already," Colavito said. "Then we shipped into the new place."

"And now we shipped back out again," snapped Ravens. As Lt. Atcheson's next-in-command, I guess he decided it was time to start assuming a bigger and bossier role.

"But what happened to Hawaii?" I pleaded. "What happened to surfing, and Maui, and Waikiki . . . ?"

"Nothing happened to them," Lt. Atcheson said. "They are right where we left them. And they'll still be there when we come back for a proper stay. Which, gentlemen, we will do."

There was grumbling and snarling all over, but nobody was moaning more than I was.

"Listen, guys," the lieutenant said, "I know you're disappointed. So am I. But you have to remember that we are part of the Armed Forces. We're here for a reason, and we serve on the orders of our superiors."

"And what are our superiors ordering us to do?" Colavito asked, in a voice just short of subordination.

"We're going to Japan," the lieutenant said. "We are going to practice maneuvers, survey beaches and underwater topography, and share our particular expertise with the Army and Marines. We are going to refine and pass on the same skills and tactics as in California, only now we're doing them in Japan."

If he was aiming to rile us up further, that was just the way to go about it. There ensued a greater level of grumbling, but to the lieutenant's credit, he let us get it out of our systems.

That took a good hour. But we did get it out.

It took much longer to get to Japan from Pearl Harbor than it had taken to get from California to Hawaii.

Possibly because one of those trips we were thrilled to be making and the other we were very much not. It felt like the early days of grade school when the teacher would haul you out of class by your ear for not even doing anything wrong.

At least, as experienced seamen, we didn't spend the journey puking this time.

And we didn't find it so bad once we got there.

The Japanese coast was vast and elegant. It didn't have the cracking surf that California did—or that Hawaii was legendary for—but the coastline was varied and the underwater even more fun to explore. There was coral that could make you forget to do your job. Once I forgot to breathe properly when a strange and exotic fish made a dramatic appearance out of the reef.

And we were doing real work here, which helped pass the time.

Based in Honsu, the largest of the Japanese islands, we spent about half our time paired up with Marines who were anxious to tap into our froggy knowledge. It wasn't the worst of duties, teaching them how to use the gear, how to navigate and map the seabed, and especially how to blow stuff up.

Then, just as this assignment was settling into a

routine that felt like a regular nine-to-five job except with flippers and explosives, everything changed entirely.

"Men," Lt. Atcheson said with more seriousness than usual. He leaned over our morning meal with his hands flat on the table. "We have been informed that the People's Army of North Korea has just crossed the thirty-eighth parallel into South Korea. They've driven the American and South Korean forces rapidly down the peninsula, and the United Nations is formulating a response as we speak.

"Gentlemen, we are at war."

CHAPTER SEVEN
Sight Unseen

Hey, Duke, wherever you are.

You said we were done with war. You said it was going to be a cushy job, more like free tourism than military service. You said I could see the world, without the world seeing me back.

Sightseeing sight unseen, you said.

You said you said you said, Duke.

And now you have got nothing to say.

Wish you were here, though. Or somewhere. Wish you were anywhere.

Didn't get to see much of your Hawaii. But I will. Then we can talk about it.

And you had better have something to say.

CHAPTER EIGHT

Via Land, Air, and Sea

Nobody knew exactly what was going to happen, but we knew something was. The intensity was ratcheted way up as we went on working for another month in Japan, readying ourselves for the big *it*, whenever it would come.

We continued training the infantry types to do what we did in the water. But one sudden difference was that we were getting extra training to do what they did as well. We spent an increasing amount of time practicing with submachine guns and pistols. This was well outside our areas of expertise, but just as the land troops seemed to relish picking up the skills of the aqua boys, I'd have to say we took pretty quickly to shooting stuff up.

We even had the privilege of Army Rangers and Scouts coming in to give us a crash course in commando tactics, hand-to-hand knife combat, martial arts—and even some helicopter and airplane recon and search and rescue.

We didn't know if we'd ever wind up using most of that stuff, but one thing was for sure: During our accelerated educational experience in Japan, our small unit of Frogmen got to be close, very fit, and about as dangerous as a bunch of amphibians could be.

Up until this point, we'd trained to travel light, silent, and quick. The only weapons we would normally carry on our missions would be our UDT-issue knife and whatever explosives we were expected to need for the job. Any other pieces of equipment we carried were for purposes of navigation, communication, or safety.

With safety being pretty much the afterthought of the equation.

But it was good to know we could handle all the other gear when called upon.

Especially since, just like that, we *were* called upon.

"All right, men," Lt. Atcheson said, gathering us in the camp's mess hall after everybody had eaten dinner. "You need to sit back down and listen up."

We'd been about to leave the hall to go to the rec building, where they were going to play the movie musical *On the Town*, with Gene Kelly. It was about three sailors on leave in New York City, and now we couldn't even get leave to the mess hall.

"Our time has come," Lt. Atcheson said.

"My time has come," Dover said, standing up from his seat, "to go see the film."

"Sit *down*, Dover," Ravens said. It looked like Dover was likely to sit down on Ravens's chest, when Lt. Atcheson gestured with two downward palms in a "sit down and calm down" motion.

"Right, then. I want everybody's undivided attention." The lieutenant leaned in close so that we were all in an intimate conversation that nobody else could be privy to. This made sense. Camp Chigasaki was actually an Army base where a tank battalion was located. I personally had no beef with the Army, but as far as a lot of the Navy was concerned, they might as well be a whole other country from us. A hostile country.

When he had that undivided attention, he let it out.

"We are mobilizing, men."

"Mobilizing where?" I said, feeling the excitement rise along with the fear.

"And when?" Chum said.

"And how?" Sheldon added.

"What are you, the Three Stooges?" Ravens snapped. "Pipe down, all of you, and let the lieutenant fill you in."

Ravens had a point. But then, so did Colavito.

"Shut up, Dogfish."

"That is enough," Lt. Atcheson growled lowly. He didn't bare his teeth often, but when he did we sat up and paid attention. "First thing tomorrow morning, we're hitching a ride on an Army troop truck. Be ready to hop off the rack, grab your bags, and move out."

He straightened up and looked us hard in the eyes, one by one. And he nodded at us, one by one.

There was nothing to do but nod back. He clearly thought he had told us something there, and of course he did, but it couldn't have been the *complete* something. Could it?

"Sir?" I said, raising my hand like a little schoolkid.

"Yes, Frew?"

"Where will the truck be headed?"

"You will know, Frew, when you need to know. As of right now, get yourselves some sleep, gentlemen. You're going to need it. Tomorrow comes early."

We made our way back to sleeping quarters while indulging in a blend of speculation, trepidation, and agitation.

"I hate not knowing," Dover said.

"Not knowing what?" Colavito said.

"Not knowing where we're going," Dover said.

"That's simple. We're going to Korea, obviously."

"How?" Dover asked. "We're going to drive there?"

"No. Probably aboard a ship. Then we'll hit the beaches of Korea the same way our guys hit the beaches of Normandy and Iwo Jima and everyplace else. Only this time, we won't stop. We'll just stomp our way northward until we eventually crash through into both China and the Soviet Union and end all this foolishness for good. To be honest, our guys really should have finished the job once we were done with Japan and Germany. Now, if we don't do the dirty work, who knows how long we'll have to be dealing with these characters?"

The whole team marched across the compound in silence for a bit. That was a lot to think about. Probably most of us were aware we would wind up in Korea. But that other stuff?

When we reached our quarters, Sheldon held the door open for the rest of us.

"Really got it all figured out, have ya, Baccala?" he asked as Colavito passed him on the way in.

"Yup," Colavito said.

"I don't want to go to China," Squid said nervously.

"You're not going to China," Sheldon said. "Relax."

"Can I go to China?" Chum asked earnestly.

"Sure," Sheldon said, "you can go."

"I'll take the Russians," Crayfish said.

"I'm with Crayfish," Muskie said.

"Right," I said, slipping through the door just in front of Sheldon, "I'll just see you boys back in Hawaii, then."

"Suit yourself," Sheldon said as the door smacked shut behind him, "but you're gonna miss all the fun."

Hmm, all the fun. It was difficult getting any serious sleep that night. I was in and out, in and out, wide awake between dreaming and thinking about all the fun.

Fits and stops chased each other in circles around my skull, like squirrels up and down a tree trunk, for six or seven hours. Finally, I greeted the first light of day. I sat up, grabbed my paper and pen, and composed an overdue note to my ma.

Hi Ma,

You should guess where I am. Or maybe you shouldn't. Sometimes these days I'm not even quite sure myself. Ah, only kidding. Sort of. Probably. Nah, definitely kidding. If you wanted to, you could find me anyway. Just follow the trail of vomit floating on the surface of the Pacific Ocean starting in San Diego Harbor headed westward.

I suppose maybe I shouldn't kid you about this stuff. I'm in Japan. They say we need to be careful about what we write home to people. Lots of top secret stuff in this business that they wouldn't want leaking out to the enemy. Not that you would leak information to the enemy, Ma, even if it was to get back at me for being a rat son some of the time. Too much of the time.

Now that I think back on it, maybe you would give information to the enemy to get back at me.

You know what? I should probably stop with the kidding. It's difficult, to be honest.

To be honest. That is what I intend. To be. To you. Honest.

I guess you heard by now that, unlike when I first signed on, there is an actual enemy and an actual war. That doesn't mean you should worry, Ma. Because you shouldn't.

Gee, this is awkward. Or I am, anyway. Just writing a letter home should not be this hard.

Well, I will be signing off now. You take care of yourself...

Just kidding again.

So listen, before I get any dumber with this, let me just try and say some things to you with some simple sentences.

I do not think I'm allowed to say where we're going. Actually, that would be hard, since I don't know myself. The important thing is, don't worry overmuch about me, because the Navy has trained me so remarkably that nothing could ever happen that I couldn't handle. Manhandle, even.

You are allowed to worry, of course, because mothers do that. That's fair and fine and reasonable. Worry. Perhaps indulge in the occasional over-worrying. But that's it. I have to draw the line if you intend to worry overmuch.

The general rule around here, Ma, is that we're not really allowed to discuss our movements. So when we're settled down in one place again, I'll write you another letter.

Meantime, Ma, I just want to say I'm sorry. You know, for all the STUFF. Whatever all the stuff was. I don't even quite know.

I bet you do, though. So, sorry.

And, I love you.

And, also, sorry.

Love,

Fergus

PS The guys call me Frogus. I hope you do not mind, because I actually like it.

I was probably the only guy who got any sleep on the transport between Camp Chigasaki and Yokota Air

Base, near Tokyo. Up front was an Army driver and his copilot, and in the back were the ten men of our outfit, bouncing around and clutching our kit bags for stability. We didn't even look exactly like Navy personnel, as by now we'd become used to our standard Army-green soldier suits, complete with the green flattop baseball caps. We did our best to settle in comfortably.

If *comfortably* was really the word to use. Our transportation was just a cross between my old Plymouth pickup and an Old West wagon, canvas cover and all.

Still, I managed to nod off probably three times in the course of the one-hour drive.

When we reached Yokota, there was something of a special occasion to it. We were hustled off the truck by a couple of Air Force guys, waving us forcefully in the direction of an aircraft that was just now spluttering into gear at our arrival.

And what a coughing beauty of a bird it was.

The PBY Catalina Flying Boat. It had twin engines, with two propellers perched on either side above the cockpit. The flight crew could look up and see their own props at about ten o'clock and two o'clock. Just in case they needed reassurance. The wing was top-mounted, which made the fuselage look even more full-bellied than it was.

We were not flight crew, however. Until further notice we were simply cargo.

"This way! This way! On you go! On you go!" barked two very serious airfield managers under the spinning propellers. The ten of us hustled, bags over our shoulders, like an army of obedient ants. We jogged from the truck to the plane, up the waiting ramp, and into the open midsection of the near-empty Catalina.

Once we had all run up and tumbled our way into the bench seats lining either side of the aircraft's rib cage, there was a mighty slam of that ramp into place. Then there was a lot of shouting from outside. The engines revved it up a good deal higher, to the point where I could see a couple of our guys trying to call out from one bench to the other but couldn't make out a word of it.

The PBY jerked forward once, then again, then again. Finally it caught some stride. Every step of the way caused more tumbling around. We were a game of Frogmen dominoes, falling sideways over one another.

After a short taxi, one more great roaring leap forward, we left the ground.

The engine noise remained deafening as we all looked around at one another. Colavito had his mouth wide open and his fists hammering excitedly on his thighs. Next to him, Dover was wide-eyed, uncertain about the great adventure we were commencing. Down the line, Squid, Chum, and Muskie all looked frozen into position, gripping their knees and staring straight ahead as if waiting for the roller coaster to come to a stop.

Along my side of the plane, Lt. Atcheson sat at the end nearest the cockpit, where the crew of three Navy pilots worked coolly, as if they did this kind of thing all the time. They probably did exactly that. Dogfish, right next to the lieutenant, had his head buried between his knees.

Crayfish, Shellfish, and yours-truly-Frogus made up the rest of our bench's lineup. All of us assumed more or less the same posture. If the wall behind us hadn't been made of good, strong, American industrial sheet metal, the three of us would have probably pushed ourselves through it by now. As it was, you could probably see the embedded shapes of our backs from the outside.

After a half hour or so, the flight of the big bird

appeared to get as stable as it was going to. At that point, Lt. Atcheson got off his seat and made his way on his knees to a spot roughly centered between the lot of us. There he stopped, addressing both sides at once.

"I'm sure you men have some ideas for where we're headed by now!" It was still loud enough that he needed to strain to be heard, but at least being heard was possible.

"China!" Colavito shouted.

"Russia!" Muskie yelled.

Atcheson turned squarely to their side of the plane and held out his hands like a traffic cop to those two on either end.

"Don't even *jokingly* talk like that!" he yelled. "That is the very type of scuttlebutt that takes on a life of its own, and the next thing you know the whole world is back at it again."

"Korea?" Dover said tentatively.

"Yes, Mr. Dover," the lieutenant said. "We are headed to Korea. But we're not flying in. We have one more connection to make along the way. Now, the reason for all the secrecy is that there's very little knowledge of our mission among the occupation personnel stationed in Japan. In fact, there's very little knowledge of it *anywhere*. Our tight little band of merry men have a particular set of skills and clandestine abilities to pull off this job without anybody being the wiser. There are very few other units—in fact, as far as I know there are none—who could accomplish what we're attempting."

I heard Crayfish yapping to Shellfish right next to me, but the words were lost.

"It means secret! Undercover!" Shelly squawked back. "Means we're good at not getting caught."

"We've got about an hour and a half before we touch down in the port of Sasebo. Sasebo is on the island of Kyushu, only about fifty miles from the city of Nagasaki. I'm sure none of you men need reminding about the significance of Nagasaki."

No, no reminders necessary. It was only five years ago that the second atomic bomb was dropped, ending the war with Japan. My first thought was wondering how safe it was to get so close now. My second thought was that it was kind of remarkable how this very journey took us through both Pearl Harbor, where a Japanese bombing had started the war for us, and Nagasaki, where an American bombing had ended it.

My third thought, following hot on the heels of the previous two, was that I sincerely hoped we weren't running that same race all over again, so close to the last one. No offense, Soviet Union and China, but it would be okay with me if Colavito was wrong and we never got to see either place up close.

"I'm sorry to say," Lt. Atcheson said, "but this is possibly your best chance to get any rest for today, so I suggest you sit back and relax as much as you can. Busy day ahead, fellas."

I would have loved to take the boss's advice, but with my skull vibrating off the hard shaking surface behind me and thoughts of the coming day ricocheting around inside, *rest* and *relax* weren't words that could apply. I managed to close my eyes now and then, but after several seconds they'd just snap back open like spring-loaded window shades.

And when they did, I found nobody else relaxing, either. To a man, we were locked in either excitement or nervousness. Muskie and Squid seemed to flicker back and forth, and Chum had a completely strange expression that I couldn't read at all.

My mind wouldn't stop racing. The thing was, looking back over our highly specific training and thinking about what the lieutenant had said about our singular suitability for this job, some conclusions were inevitable.

So just how cold *was* the water off the Korean coast?

The big, rumbly PBY made even more noise as it lowered itself down from the sky than it had made climbing up. As it did, and as we got closer to everything we were about to face, I could feel my heart rate accelerating, my stomach fluttering, adrenaline trying to make fire hoses out of both ears.

"Hang on, men!" Lt. Atcheson roared, because he is a good leader rather than because any of us needed reminding.

But we did hang on harder than before. And good thing, too.

Roooooarrrr! Bam! Bam! B-bammm . . .

We were all reminded that one of the defining features of the amphibious PBY—the "Flying Boat"—was that it was a seaplane. That great, broad belly of hers was shaped like a shallow-draft boat hull for good reason.

"Wa-hoooooo!" Colavito hollered. Water washed over the sides of the plane. We could feel it under the boat and could see it in the glass of the cockpit. The flight crew reacted not at all. A bunch of our guys joined in the woo-hooing before Lt. Atcheson finally reacted out of pure embarrassment.

"For goodness' sake, act like you are in the United States Navy," he growled.

"Yeah," Dogfish added, though as the engines cut out and the plane started rocking in all directions, he put his head quietly back down.

Only a few minutes later, the side of the plane opened up. We were directed to come out in single file, onto the ramp.

The next leg of our adventure floated approximately thirty yards beyond it.

Getting to our Higgins boat, however, required a small shuttle.

I was the first man down the plane's ramp. My sea legs were wobbly to the point where I actually toddled the whole way with the aid of two sailors from the waiting inflatable raft. I went right over the side and landed on my chest on the bottom. Shellfish then landed on top of me, followed by what felt like Crayfish on top of both of us.

We were immediately rowed across to the Higgins boat, before the raft went back for the other guys.

It couldn't have been more than ten minutes total between when the Flying Boat hit the water, the rubber boat began the shuttle, and the Higgins boat slammed right into flank speed.

It was like we were getting the crash tour of how to get from A to B to C in the modern US Navy.

It was all happening at such velocity that I mostly just hung over the side of the Higgins like a dog out of a car window.

For the first time, we could actually see our destination *before* boarding it in a mad, awful hurry. There, floating serenely on the horizon, was a Green Dragon.

CHAPTER NINE

What the Tide Brought In

Green Dragons were destroyers that were specifically converted to support amphibious operations. Much of their armament had been removed or refitted to accommodate various smaller boats and landing craft in their configuration. They got their nickname from the green, swirly camouflage design of their paint job—which had to be the Marines' idea, since the Raiders made regular use of them.

Getting us all on board was as taxing as any part of the day so far. The Higgins pulled alongside the destroyer, where we were required to sling our bags over our backs, make it onto the climbing net that had been dropped for us, and then scale the side of the undulating ship.

By the time we'd all slung up over the side, there wasn't a one of us who was not standing wobbly-legged and thanking our lucky stars for the insanely rigorous physical training we had been put through for all those months.

We were shown to our quarters and then taken to the mess for some welcome nourishment. After dinner, we were told we had another ritzier mess meeting to attend. We were summoned to the officers' mess, which was a rare privilege for lowly amphibians like ourselves and likely to be the only time any of us would ever get inside one of those fancy little restaurants.

As it turned out, it was all about business.

There were a lot of materials that were waiting on the ship when we arrived: photographic recon, charts of coastal waters, maps, and the like. Lt. Atcheson went right to work as soon as we got there, with the captain and the rest of the ship's brass taking a back seat to look on as he did.

"Okay, men, our objective is clear. We are to slip into this harbor here." He pointed to a spot on the east coast, clearly on the north side of the Korean divide. "There is a very important and busy railway line that the North Koreans are using extensively to supply their drive into the South. Interdiction here is critical. We'll slow their advances to buy our side more time to produce men and firepower. Enough to give them a proper fight. Which, frankly, we're not managing to do at the moment."

The bunch of us remained silent, looking up and down over the picture as it was being presented to us.

"Now, I don't want to overburden you with excess pressure," the lieutenant continued, "and I wouldn't chance this mission if I didn't think—if I didn't *know*—you were equipped to handle it. So I'll give it to you straight. What we're being asked to do is risky and complicated. There's no playbook here. I suppose you could say that's why *we* are being asked to do it. The sum total of our trained Underwater Demolition Team experts are in this room right now."

There was a statement to get the guys' attention.

I appreciated everything the lieutenant was saying to us. And the thoughtful way he was saying it. But it occurred to me that if he wanted to give it to us straight, like he said, he was doing it in a kind of roundabout way.

"Lieutenant?" I asked with my now standard schoolboy raised hand.

"Yes, Frew?"

"What *is* it we're being asked to do?"

"Oh, right," he said, in an unusually absentminded way. "We are to infiltrate this harbor, locate and identify the critical points of the rail line and bridge . . . and blow them out of service."

The first reaction to this satisfyingly straight-forward explanation was an eruption of cheers from the men, though on a lower scale than usual. We instinctively knew not to erupt in an officers' mess the way we would have in the regular world. After all, the *D* in our UDT designation was *demolition*. This was what we trained for. This was what we were waiting for.

"Excuse me," Dover said, with his just-so balance of respect and curiosity.

"Yes?" Lt. Atcheson said.

"Is this a train that runs through the water?"

Ah. Navy UDTs also had that *U* as a fundamental part of their identity.

Lt. Atcheson inhaled and exhaled calmly.

"No," he said. "It does not run through water. But it does run very, very *close by* the water. Our areas of expertise are expanding. We're being asked to do what we do best: swimming, diving, scouting, demolishing. But we're now being asked to take those skills onto dry land as well. Because frankly, men, there will be times, like now, when we'll be the only game in town. And you know what? The reality is that we can blow up any*thing*, any *time*, with or without the help of the Army or the Marines, or anybody else."

Once more, Lt. Atcheson displayed his gift for knowing his audience. Despite the fact that we had never trained for this combination of unaided sea-and-shore attack, every member of the team instantly dropped any reservations and growled approval.

The lieutenant, obviously buoyed by that response, leaned back into the maps and charts, and the task of showing us what it all meant.

We lay quietly in our bunks, hoping for sleep more than expecting it.

"I really wanted to see that movie," Dover finally said to nobody.

"What movie?" Crayfish asked.

"*On the Town*," Dover answered. "It would have been fun to watch a film about sailors on leave."

"I don't know," said Colavito. "I haven't seen it, but I'm betting it isn't the best sailors-on-leave movie out there. Not even the best sailors-on-leave *musical*. Not even the best sailors-on-leave musical *with Gene Kelly* in it."

"Oh, come on, Baccala," I said, since he clearly had this routine all thought out. "Spit it out already."

"*Anchors Aweigh* would have to be better."

"And why would it have to be better?" asked Sheldon, as if he was seriously delving for information.

"Because Frank Sinatra has top billing in *Anchors Aweigh.*"

That prompted a sea of groans. Nobody anywhere liked washed-up old Frank Sinatra anymore.

"Yeah?" Colavito said, sounding genuinely offended. "Well, my pop says Gene Kelly can't sing for beans."

"And who's your father?" Dover asked. "Some kind of talent scout or something?"

"No," Colavito said seriously. "But he's Italian."

The half of us who thought that was intended as a joke laughed tentatively, while the ones who weren't sure didn't. Then Baccala himself broke the tie by spluttering out a good, harsh laugh. Then everybody joined in. And it felt good.

The conversations went more or less like that for the next hour, stories from back home when we were kids, about surfing wipeouts where guys lost their shorts in the wave, dumb jokes about armadillos and patent-leather shoes. Anything that distracted us from where we were going and what we were doing. Even the bravest among us, undoubtedly Colavito, was scared.

The knuckleheadery of our stories carried us until something like sleep descended.

Morning, as they liked to say in the Armed Services, came early.

It was just about one a.m. when Lt. Atcheson and his flunky-monkey Dogfish marched into our quarters and rousted us out of the racks. As the lieutenant humanely shook me and then Sheldon awake, Dogfish was working the other side of the room. There was groaning, yawning, and grumbling, and I distinctly heard Dover say to Dogfish, "Buddy, the first person I kill in this job is gonna be you."

The destroyer was still running flat out—nearly thirty knots—as we got up to the supply store on the top deck and started preparing for the raid. Because of the night maneuver and in-and-out nature of the assault, we were all covering our faces and hands in the dark green camouflage grease paint normally associated with jungle commandos. The fact that the weather in Korea in August didn't differ much from my home waters off the Southern California coast meant there was not a lot of complication to the gear we would be wearing. Most of the guys were sporting the same green infantry-type outfits we normally wore. Their jobs were going to be handling the explosives, which would require no specialty equipment. But the two lead scout swimmers—the best swimmers on the team—were Muskie and me. We were dressed in the warm-weather outfits of shorts and T-shirts, with a knife strapped to one hip and an all-purpose coil of rope strapped to the other. We, like everybody else, were supplied with M3 ("the Greaser") submachine guns strapped to our backs. Unlike everybody else, however, Muskie and I pulled on these booties, sort of like heavy-grade rubber socks, that we would later put our froggy flippers over.

Most importantly, each man was responsible for collecting one sixty-pound pack of explosives, then loading them onto the boat destined for the harbor.

That boat, the same LCP(R) that collected us off the plane, was now idling on the port side of the ship. It had been modified with sound mufflers underneath and two 30-caliber machine guns mounted in the turrets on either side of the cockpit. The guns were a crisp reminder that this was no ordinary surf outing we were embarking on. Three of the destroyer crew were already in position on the LCP(R), while several more got together to heave our ten-man inflatable boat over the side and into the lapping waters below. The gunners attached the inflatable to the LCP(R) and then signaled for the bunch of frogs to hop on down.

It took about a half hour to get all ten of the UDT crew, with their bundles of TNT, down and onto the boat. It took about half a second for the pilot of that boat to rip into high gear and get us racing in the direction of the Democratic People's Republic of Korea.

Another half hour of the LCP(R) skipping across the thankfully calm surface of the Sea of Japan, and suddenly the engine shifted downward. All of our guys—who were squatted down along the perimeter wall of the boat—hopped up and looked over the sides like a colony of prairie dogs.

There it was. The Korean coast. Though it was dark, we could still make it out across the flat sea: the easy-lying beach and formidable rocky uplands beyond. Somehow, it seemed to me like an appropriate representation of the task—of this mission and everything beyond it. A simple approach with a steeply graduating degree of difficulty beyond.

"This is jump-off," the pilot of the boat called to Lt. Atcheson.

"Right," the lieutenant responded, all business. Then he gestured to his guys—us—to get the stuff and get over the side. We were decamping to the rubber boat that would take us simply and silently into the harbor roughly a mile away.

Once our team and our gear was all aboard, the LCP(R) pilot informed Lt. Atcheson, "We'll be just out here, making half-mile circuits, waiting for your signal. At which time, we will come racing in to pick you boys up. Be *ready* to be picked up, or be ready to swim your way home. Got it?"

"Got it," Lt. Atcheson said, but in a tone that was far less respectful than the words.

"Break a leg, boys," the pilot called out. The landing craft took off, and we commenced rowing toward shore.

It was hard work, despite the all-hands-on-deck nature of our rowing. And looking around the boat in the minimal light, I had to say we looked like a pretty impressive, almost frightening outfit. With our green greasy grimace faces, our muscles straining, and armed to the bulging eyeballs with both destructive capability and willpower, this was a group I personally would not want to mess with.

Even if, inside, we were all witless with anxiety.

When we finally approached the break line, I felt both apprehension and nostalgia. And a heaviness in my heart. It made me think of simpler days out surfing at

San Onofre, paddling past the line to wait for just the perfect wave. Waiting, floating, by myself. Back when "by myself" was an actual, possible something.

Sometimes, back then, I would simply float, ride up and down on the swells, just because that alone felt so good. I'd even let good waves—pretty, delicious waves—go unchallenged. Riding the swell, beyond the reach of the whole world, was satisfying enough.

And Duke. Duke was the heart heaviness. It reminded me of the break line, just beyond which Duke—the Duke who steered me to this situation, this place, this existence—went below the surface and never again came up for life.

"Frew!" Lt. Atcheson hissed urgently in my face. Apparently I'd missed my cue to go overboard with Muskie. We had managed to get the inflatable over the break line and into the whitewater. The boat now bobbed and fought the modest but persistent wave action, through the efforts of a well-coordinated team of paddlers. The two advance scouts needed to get a move on.

The lieutenant strapped the last of my gear onto my belt: a plastic-wrapped pack of plastic explosives, complete with detonator cord and mini plunger; four grenades, also secured in plastic; and a waterproofed walkie-talkie. These items were strung to the waist belt with a trailing line that allowed them to float along behind the Frogmen, to be collected and employed when needed.

His impatience growing, the lieutenant fairly heaved me into the water.

Muskie and I commenced the swim to shore, knowing that the job the guys were doing behind us was probably even tougher. The waves kept trying to drive them toward the beach, while they tried to paddle back toward the breaker line but not beyond it. It would take a lot of effort for them to keep that boat, and all its concentrated explosives, in almost exactly the same spot until we sent them the signal that it was all clear to come on in and blow the place to smithereens.

I always wanted to know exactly what *smithereens* were, and I was hoping this was my night to find out.

It was a cloudless, starry night, and it wasn't hard to look up and feel the warm weightlessness, as if we were a part of the sky. It also wasn't hard to look down and be instantly pulled back into the seriousness of the task at hand.

"You okay?" I said quietly, pulling up alongside Muskie.

"Nervous," he said in return.

"Then you're okay," I said. "Because if you weren't nervous, you'd be crazy."

"Thanks," he said, and we said no more.

After several minutes of stealthy swimming, adding barely any ripples of our own to the calm but insistent surf, Muskie and I beached.

And encountered our first unexpected complication. Undoubtedly there would be more, as we were trained to always figure on them.

The beach itself was small, not much more than a shallow spit of sand that could serve as a slipway for one boat. And that spit of sand butted right up against a sea wall. Thirty feet of cliff ledge stood between us and the train tunnel. We could see everything as we made our way in, but the wall was so high that when we came right up to it, we couldn't even see where the tunnel was.

"What now?" Muskie asked me.

I scanned up and down as best I could in the dark and noticed the ledge tapered away off to our right, where it came up against a natural rock formation in the water. I motioned to Muskie that we should head that way to find an accessible spot.

We deposited our flippers there in the sand and gathered up our tow lines, with the explosive materials attached.

Basically, we followed our noses and the line of the coast until we came to those rocks. Then we scrambled for a while more to find an access point that would be reasonably easy to negotiate without risking our necks any more than we were already risking them.

Time and tension were ticking ever louder until we saw our chance. Muskie was feeling it every bit as much as I was, and he climbed over me to get to the spot where the rocks were built like a giant's stepladder up along the side of the railway tunnel. The two of us crept rodent-like along the wall for a couple minutes until we were just beside the point where the tracks shot out of the tunnel, rolling parallel with the water.

"I think it's time to call the boys in," Muskie said to me.

I agreed and worked to disengage my clunky two-way radio. There was some water in the bag, but the unit itself was built to put up with a certain amount of that. I flicked the switch, then fiddled with the dial to listen for the squelch.

No squelch.

"What's the matter?" Muskie asked.

"I don't know," I said. I turned the radio around and around in my hands, looking for answers to explain the dead air.

And I found one. At the heel of the unit, the plate that held the batteries in place had come slightly undone. It wasn't screwed together tightly enough, and so it got itself all salt waterlogged.

"Nothing?" Muskie asked, with just a little desperation because I had gone all stupid and failed to fill him in.

"Yeah, radio's dead," I said.

"Now what?"

"I'm going to have to swim back out to tell them to come in here."

He went silent for several seconds. It was dark enough that reading his expression in the absence of words meant I had to get my face right up close to see it.

I found him chewing his bottom lip. His eyebrows traveled up and down his forehead like he had no control over them.

"Gimme your pack," he said finally.

"What?" I said.

"Your TNT pack. Hand it over. I'll start setting

charges while you go out and bring the rest of the team in."

Go, Muskie! I quickly brought out my explosives and fuse cord, handed them over, and gave him a fairly hard chuck on the shoulder for his efforts.

"Hey!" he hissed. "You want to blow me up before we can get the other guys?"

"Sorry," I said, and took off back along the tunnel wall, to the rocks, to the beach, and back into my flippers.

I threw myself straight into the water, without my explosives or my partner, but still with my knife on my hip, my grenade pack trailing behind me, and my M3 on my back.

Enough to make me feel like a United States Navy fighting man.

I pumped hard, straight into the waves, and felt again something like my old self in the surf of San Onofre. Only armed and dangerous this time.

The guys seemed to be struggling, but winning in their battle to keep the raft in place. I was about fifty yards away from them when somebody spotted me and that was all the sign they needed. They started paddling immediately, but they weren't as fast as I was.

I shot through the water like a marlin, determined not to leave Muskie on his own for one second more than necessary. I felt at this point like I already knew this piece of planet Earth as well as anyplace I had ever mapped out in my head. I took it for granted that the boatful of frogs could just follow me and everything would fall into place.

I hit the beach and shed the fins like a tadpole gaining his legs. Without losing momentum I ran along the sand to the point in the rocks we had found the first time. I had this feeling now like I could do all this blindfolded and still get it right— which was almost true in the depth of night we were covered in.

It could not have been more than a couple of minutes before I reached the mouth of the tunnel again.

To find no Muskie.

My first reaction was panic. My chest heaved as I found myself hyperventilating. I put my palms flat on either side of my rib cage and compressed, to get the unhelpful panting to stop. It worked, well enough and quick enough for me to be able to get spooked all over again.

Running footsteps came charging up behind me.

I dropped to one knee and spun around, simultaneously grabbing my M3 off my back.

"Don't" was all Colavito said as he threw himself down next to me.

"Holy smokes," I said, using my elbows now to compress my rib cage.

Nothing doing, this time. I was just going to have to pant because a ruckus kicked off deep inside the tunnel, where Muskie must have decided to place the first charges. There was screaming and shouting, and it wasn't in English, so Korean was the logical next guess. Then there was the *rattatattatatta* of machine gun fire and all kinds of pained screaming.

Then, as Colavito and I ran out and squared up at the mouth of the tunnel, Muskie came flying out like an Olympic sprinter—if the Olympics included an event where you sprinted in one direction and tossed a grenade back in the other.

Bu-hooom! came the reverb of racket exploding all around the tunnel.

As Muskie passed us by, Baccala and I sprayed the cave with machine-gun fire for several seconds, before bolting back in the direction of the exit route.

Muskie must have decided he didn't have time for that.

"Go, go, go, go!" he shouted in the direction of the team, as he continued running full-speed toward and over the seawall.

We heard the large and pained scream as he hit the water, then muffled voices from the guys for mere seconds before they shoved off.

Colavito and I made it to the rocks. As we looked back toward the track, we saw an old-fashioned hand-car pumping out of the tunnel. Two North Korean soldiers jumped off and ran to the edge of the seawall, firing in the direction of our guys with machine guns that looked surprisingly like our own.

We rather wisely decided we would leave two perfectly good pairs of flippers on the beach.

The boat was just about to clear the break line when we dove in. Frogus and Codfish swam like the natural water babies we were, straight out to sea.

The *ping, splish, kerspling* of bullets plunking in the water all around us as we hacked our way through the tide sounded a lot like tossing pebbles into a lake, except for the fact that it was completely terrifying.

Fortunately, as great a thing as the submachine gun

can be when you need it, long-range shooting is not its strongest point.

We were out of harm's way at just about the same time we were out of arm strength. So it was a pretty good thing that the boys in the inflatable stopped to wait for us only a hundred yards beyond the break line.

"That was fun," Baccala said as we dog-paddled toward them for collection.

"I wish I had the strength to drown you right now," I said, my chest heaving away.

"Ha! You'll *never* have that strength, kid."

CHAPTER TEN

Break a Leg

Nobody did break a leg.

Muskie, however, broke two ankles in his fall.

It was getting light out when the LCP(R) delivered us back to the destroyer. As we pulled up, there was a Coast Guard Flying Boat waiting to collect Muskie and carry him off to the hospital. Lt. Atcheson had given him something for the pain, and he looked kind of groggy there, lying flat on his bed of high explosives.

"Did we get 'em?" he asked.

"Hard to tell," I said.

"How many were on the handcar coming out of the tunnel?" he asked as the Coast Guard medics boarded our boat to collect their patient.

"Two," I said.

The medics picked him up by the arms and legs, and he just closed his eyes and started chuckling.

"How many were there inside the tunnel?" I asked.

"Six," he said, laughing like a man in no pain at all.

As the two medics on our boat coordinated with two more on the Flying Boat to get our hero aboard, the whole team of frogs broke into wild cheers, whistles, and woofs. I believe there was even a ribbit or two thrown in.

For the next five weeks or so, we took our experience from that first raid and refined our skills. We got to the point where, if we decided something needed to be blown up, it usually got blown up.

We traveled up and down the east coast of the Korean Peninsula, along the south coast, and then up and down the west. As far as living conditions were concerned, we were quite the amphibious vagabonds. We would spend a week aboard the destroyer, then camp out on one of the offshore islands. We'd make a raid, get back onto the destroyer for a week, then swim out for more. The best part, though, was when we steamed back to Japan for restocking and relaxing at the base in Yokosuka.

More underwater demolition personnel were arriving in the Far East regularly now. And technically, our team was growing. But as far as I was concerned—and it was a feeling shared by most of the guys—our little detachment of ten men, now nine, was our team.

It was simply in the nature of our work that we were never going to be part of a brigade or battalion. We were happily in the service of our American and United Nations fighters everywhere. Like true amphibians, we could enter any formation, but we existed as our own pod, functioned as our own single organism.

That may have sounded a little light on camaraderie, but it worked brilliantly from our perspective. And as for me personally, it was about ten times as much camaraderie as I'd ever managed before.

Son,

There is no need, ever, for you to apologize to me. Even at your worst...and your worst can be rather harsh, as you know...I never stopped knowing who you are on the inside. And that inside version of you is somebody I couldn't possibly love more. It was just that he was trapped within the cold fish you were on the outside.

See, you aren't the only one who can play at that jokester game.

In all seriousness, though, you could be quite a rotter at times.

But I knew what you were going through. Of course I did. Because I was going through it as well. My job was just to wait for you to break past that wave and surface again.

I've gotten good at waiting.

Which is fortunate, since you've got me doing it again, haven't you?

But I don't mind. As long as this time, at the end of it, the service sends my man back home whole.

They will do that, right? Tell me they will do that.

If they ask you to do anything dangerous, you just tell them that your mother says no. But keep your manners. You have fine manners, one of the many things that make me proud of you. So proud, Fergus. And if you tell them no, firmly yet politely, I am sure they will give you no trouble.

And if they need a note from your mother, you can show them this one. If that's not good enough, then I will break out the good stationery and really show them a thing or two.

I have not lost my mind. I know you have to do dangerous things. I may, however, lose my mind if anything happens to you.
Take every care, my son. Must go now.
Love, Ma

"Hey, everybody, Fergus is cryin'. Come see this! It's adorable."

Chum the Dumb was speaking. He had somehow managed to slip over and worm his way beside me on my bunk while I read my mail. Chum wasn't an awful guy, but he wasn't much *good*, either. Up until now his defining characteristics were general uselessness and a pleased fascination with his own appearance. He had a deep-cloven chin dimple like Kirk Douglas, and every time he passed a reflective surface he would stare and trace it with his finger, like, *How did that get there?*

"Don't waste your time, guys," I called out to the rest of my bunkmates. "I'm not crying, my eyes are sweating."

That was good enough to earn some chuckles among the guys, who were busy reading letters of their own. Which left me free to turn my attention on Chum.

"If you don't get off my bed right now, *you'll* be crying—so hard the whales will call back in response."

I was promptly allowed to resume my own company. No hard feelings, but Chum's relationship with Chum was such that he never developed proper interpersonal skills. So this was his idea of banter.

That was about as bad as relations on the team would get, though. Which wasn't bad at all, considering the close quarters and working conditions we had to endure. The interdependence and trust required to do our jobs meant that we all had a greater stake in getting along than in not.

Except the one time. In spite of all that, or possibly because of it, tension rose to such a boil that a couple of us just had to settle it for good.

We were back at our home base at Yokosuka. Summer was turning to autumn, and we were turning from rookies to something a bit harder and more seasoned. As the weather cooled, we did more of our training in our cold-water dry suits, appropriately looking more and more like actual frogs all the time. Finally, for the first time in ages, Lt. Atcheson announced at the end of breakfast one morning that we should spend a half day doing absolutely nothing. Swimming, fishing, high-diving into the bay—or even just eating. He didn't care, as long as we enjoyed ourselves.

This, naturally, was a very popular proclamation.

And so it was decidedly unpopular when somebody gummed up the works.

"Lieutenant," Dogfish helpfully objected.

"Yes, Ravens?" the lieutenant said.

Dogfish Ravens proceeded to remind our boss that we were still scheduled to complete the last little task left undone on our training itinerary: the gas chamber.

Also known as the Confidence Chamber.

I had enough confidence already, thank you very much. On account of all the other stuff we'd been through, crucibles that most people in the world would never see.

Lt. Atcheson, being the stand-up guy that he was, responded, "I think I can do without taking the men through the chamber, Ravens. Especially in light of all the trials by fire they've already endured."

"Oh, I'll take them, sir," Ravens said cheerily.

Bless him, the lieutenant kept trying. "We don't even know whether the base's chamber is—"

"It's available, sir," Dogfish piped up. "I've checked, and we can have it this morning if we like."

If we like. Like?

Lt. Atcheson looked around at the lot of us as we looked sadly back at him. His face said: *Look, I tried, guys.*

"Well," the lieutenant said, "we *are* all supposed to experience this. And it's a good thing to have under your belt . . ."

Right next to me was Baccala, and next to him was Dogfish. That was plenty close enough to hear the exchange.

"I am gonna *kill* you," Colavito said hoarsely.

"Oh no you're not," Ravens said with a careless waving away of the words.

"Oh yes I am," Colavito reassured him.

Now, in the Armed Forces, and in the lives of young men generally, it's not uncommon to hear one soldier say something like *I'm going to kill you* to another. Under normal circumstances, you aren't expected to take the words literally.

Under these very circumstances, it was hard to take them any other way.

The Confidence Chamber was a concrete block of a room, ten feet by ten. The whole team of us was herded in, and the door was slammed behind us. We all wore our gas masks. There was one thick, small observation window where a trained technician oversaw the operation, with the soon-to-be-dead Dogfish watching us from over his shoulder.

Once we were all inside, nice and snug, the room began to fill up with a smoky-looking gas.

There was also an intercom system. When the room was filled so densely with tear gas that our masks fogged over completely, a voice—Ravens's—started calling out names in the order we were supposed to remove our masks.

"Clayton," he called out, and Crayfish duly removed his mask. We all stood around watching, first in solidarity, then when he did not seem to suffer, in relief. Then his eyes bugged out a bit. He started wheezing. We had to keep clearing the glass visors of our masks to watch as poor Crayfish dropped his mask, bent over, and put his hands on his knees for support.

Various fluids started streaming down from his face to the floor.

"Chamberlain!" Ravens called out.

Chum turned and looked to the little window as if challenging Ravens. *What, this applies to me?*

"Chamberlain!" came the call again.

Chum tore off his mask petulantly. Then he stood, looking around with his hands on his hips, like it was a piece o' cake.

Which lasted maybe fifteen seconds.

Chum made a lot more noise than Crayfish had, actually screaming instead of gasping. He started clawing at his own eyes, as if that would make anything better. When he dropped to his knees, he was spitting violently, like a colony of fire ants had gotten in there.

"Chilton!" came the next call, and Squid didn't waste any time. He tore off the mask and threw it straight up into the air so that it fell immediately back to Earth and conked him on the head. He fell to the floor and promptly started producing a small lake of drool on the floor between his hands.

"Dover, Sheldon, Frew!" the sadistic Dogfish called out in rapid succession.

The three of us peeled back our masks and gave dignity our best shot. We looked back and forth among ourselves, hoping to sustain strength in numbers. We watched the tears first well, then spray out of our eyes. Shelly looked at me pleadingly, as if there was anything I could do. Dover shook his head around like a maniac, the way a hunting dog does when he's got something in his jaws that he would like to kill. The drool I saw out of the mouths of those two stout fighting men would have embarrassed a baby.

My eyes burned as if there was actual fire applied to them. I tried holding them tightly closed, then putting my hands over them, then opening them up again, then fanning them with both my hands.

But nothing worked. Eventually we fell to our knees like the others.

"Colavito!" Dogfish called out.

Baccala had been made to watch the whole lot of us suffer what he would have to endure. This was no accident. If it was me, I would have found last-man-called to be the most excruciating position of all, despite getting to spend the least amount of time in the actual tear gas.

Somehow, I didn't think Colavito cared one bit whether he was first or last or anywhere in between.

I was on my back by this point, writhing around. Not that I had any choice in the matter, but I discovered that this was probably the best place, both to breathe properly and to see what was going on around me.

Colavito stood there, maskless. He blinked a little. Then he blinked a lot. Then he bent over and propped himself with his hands on his knees for several seconds. Then he straightened up again. His face looked a mess, like the rest of us. Tears streamed out of his crazed, puffy eyes. But he wasn't giving in. Then came the drool. He didn't fight it. In fact, he treated it like another welcome challenge. He opened his broad Baccala mouth and allowed the saliva to well up and pour over his bottom lip like some kind of public fountain.

Then, best of all, he walked on slightly wobbly legs right up to the little observation window.

He raised his hand and, with his palm facing upward and his four fingers flapping, he made the "come on" gesture to the guy on the other side of the glass.

And he did not mean the technician.

In just a few seconds, and very much to his credit, Dogfish burst through the door into the chamber of horrors with the rest of us suffering, squirming frogs. By then, Colavito was doing well just to remain upright, but he didn't have much left. Ravens, who had already been through this in his own previous training, slammed the door behind him and stood at attention, as if this was just a normal, fresh-air review.

It was impressive, which wasn't something we would normally have associated with BM3 Ravens.

He still looked the part as Colavito staggered up to him, looked in his sneering, smiling face . . . and belted him with an overhand cross that was as likely to drill him into the floor as knock him out.

The two of them proceeded to hammer away at each other with a vengeance, in a scene unlikely to have ever occurred before in any Confidence Chamber. The rest of us attempted to jump in and break up the fight, but the gas took care of that impulse. All we could do was scramble to our feet and then tumble back down again, writhing all over one another like fishing worms in a gigantic can.

Then, with a loud pop, the doors at either end of the chamber shot open, the gas started seeping out, and the frogs followed close behind.

It took ages for us to get our composure back again. The gas clung to our clothes as well as all the soft tissue it had already attacked within our sinuses, throats, and lungs.

Like true warriors, however, Colavito and Ravens continued wailing away at each other until the rest of us got ourselves together enough to simply tackle them into submission on the corridor floor.

"So, what have we got here?" Lt. Atcheson asked, when the group of us reconvened for lunch. Most of us looked like a bunch of pink-eyed, drooly crybabies.

Dogfish had a black eye, a bisected right eyebrow, and a bottom lip so thoroughly split you could park your bicycle in it and it wouldn't tip over.

Colavito was showing the boss a mouth with one fewer teeth than he'd showed him at breakfast.

"We have a unit that has most ably completed the last of their training requirements, Lieutenant," Ravens said stoically.

The lieutenant smiled and nodded individually at each of us.

"To think," he said, "I tried to talk you out of it."

Ravens had held his own. He didn't take nearly as bad a beating as we all would have expected. He lost a fight, but he gained a lot more in that Confidence Chamber.

CHAPTER ELEVEN
Lung Capacity

As summer turned definitively to autumn, the air and water temperature cooled steadily, and it was time for us to get used to the cold-water gear that made us look truly like frogs.

Every dress-up was a two-man job.

"Are you putting on weight?" Dover asked me, with a poke in the ribs for emphasis. As my dressing partner, he was around the back of me, helping me gear up for another night raid to create havoc on a busy Communist-controlled port. We were on the top deck of our current Amphibious Personnel Destroyer (APD), with the boats already loaded and waiting down in the water portside.

I was well aware that I was not putting on weight. In fact, I'd been getting thinner, as the bosses kept us busy on constant missions along the coast. So Dover's question required a succinct answer.

"Shut up, frog-face."

"I'm just saying!" He laughed as he pulled the two back flaps of my rubber suit tightly together. "You're looking a little fuller, that's all."

I turned crisply, spun him around, then muscled him into his own dry suit. Then the two of us were lowered down on a rope, the last of the team to get there. By the time we hit the LCP(R), the rubber boat had already been latched to the side. The rest of the guys were strapping on their knives, ropes, and guns. We all had our flippers on already, and half had affixed their underwater masks.

We absolutely did look like frogs.

The pilot ripped into flank speed, and we scooted across the water to the drop-off spot, a mile from shore. There was another train track, and a rail bridge that led right up to the supply depot. Intelligence had identified the spot as being crammed full of weapons, ammunition, and explosives. The beauty was that if we could do a quick hit and set a minimum of charges, the target would pretty much blow *itself* into the sky. The less beauteous part was that if we made any mistakes while we were in there, we'd end up headed skyward along with it.

Unlike some of our raids, this one was not going to involve scout swimmers ahead of a rubber boat full of

TNT. We were traveling light. A fraction of the fire-power could get this job done, and chances were about even that the place would be well defended. Traveling light and fast was key.

So the landing craft was depositing us all straight into the water, and we would make our way in under our own power. As we reached the perfect point, we went in pairs over the side of the LCP(R) and into the rubber boat. After a quick ride, we slowed down only a little at the lieutenant's signal. The first man tumbled, backward, into the water. Fifty feet farther along, the second man went in. Two guys then replaced those two in the rubber boat and *plunk*, *plunk*, in they went.

Dover and I were now in the rubber boat, bouncing along the choppy surface of the water. Then Dover was over.

Another fifty feet, and in I went.

I immediately righted myself and started heading for shore. I checked my instruments. On one wrist, I wore the watch Ma had gotten me. On the other, I had the Navy-issue compass and the depth gauge, which let us know if fear or disorientation had caused us to hang too long, too far under the surface. The compass and watch were more important. They would

162

be required in order to get back to the exact spot where each of us was dropped off, and at the appointed time.

I knew I wasn't going to go too deep, and my lungs told me when I was hanging under the surface too long. It was easily over three minutes of swimming before I felt the need to come up for air. By the time I did, I was so far into shore I could see the white sand of the beach even with no moonlight. I could also see at least two of the guys scrambling up that beach.

Dover and I were still at least a couple of minutes from joining in all the fun. But we knew how much damage even one half of a detachment of amphibious demolition experts could do in two minutes.

Not wanting to be late for the party, I put my head down and started pumping double speed for the shore.

By the time I raised my head out of the water again, I was practically on top of the beach.

I started climbing up from the gentle surf when a chaotic blast of gunfire and screaming drowned out any sounds of the sea.

I was standing there on one leg like a glistening green flamingo, having just gotten one flipper off. Then there was a firm hand on my arm as Dover insisted, "Come on, come on, come on!" He yanked me hard enough that I stumbled into the shallows, then bounded right back up with one flipper in my hand and the other still on my foot.

Our orders were very clear on this: If discovered, we were to pull out immediately. We were not infantry.

Dover and I created more splash than we would have liked as we hopped into the sea. Once under the water, I managed to get my flipper back on and avoid the possibility of just swimming myself in a little circle until somebody shot me.

Which was a real possibility. As I started pumping through the incoming tide I heard one muffled *kerplunk* to my left, and then another to my right, as bullets bracketed my exit from this most unfriendly port.

We chugged for open water, my heart and lungs feeling like the engine room of a tugboat. But I was for certain swimming faster than any old tug ever could.

I was also petrified thinking about the fate of the other guys, since there was no way of telling who was where at this point. My only job now, my only training for this moment, was getting back out to the exact spot where the boat had dropped me off.

It comforted me in the moment, to think that made me just like a salmon, returning to the spot where it was born in order to breed the next generation into being.

I could be as smart as a fish, I thought. And so could the rest of the guys.

Bu-hoooom! One tremendous explosion snapped me out of my fish dream, followed by two more: *Bu-hooom . . . Bu-hooom.*

I wanted to stop, to turn around and examine the beauty of what we could do, what we may have done.

But we weren't trained to watch. We were trained to swim, to demolish, and to swim away again.

So I swam.

After I reached my coordinates, I hung there kicking my fins and treading water with my rubber-gloved hands for probably twenty minutes. Finally I saw the pickup boat making a big, graceful arc inland.

The arc ended at just about the spot where Dover should have been. I got myself ready, because this was one of the most thrilling and precise of all our oft-practiced maneuvers. It was essentially the same deal as when we were dropped off, only in reverse. And with a much higher degree of difficulty.

The boat comes swiftly along and the guys hope to find you right where you're supposed to be. If they don't find you there, tough luck, they have to keep going to find guys who have done it right. I could tell by the action of the boat that they'd just picked up Dover, and so I readied myself.

They were looking right down the line to my spot when the lieutenant lurched over the side of the boat with the pickup loop—which is like a large fishing net but without the net. I did my bit by raising one arm straight up.

The lieutenant reached out and scooped me up, exactly the way you would to bring in a big fish. The momentum of the maneuver, combined with the speed of the boat, lifted me up and flung me in one smooth motion into the rubber boat behind Lt. Atcheson.

The lieutenant yanked the loop back over my head and poised himself over the side again to catch the next fish. Meanwhile, Dogfish grabbed and bundled me up over the side of the rubber raft and into the LCP(R) to make room. I tumbled over and right into Dover.

The two of us stood straight up, watching for the next guys to come back aboard.

Where the next guy should have been, there was nobody. The pilot briefly throttled the engine down, as we all peered around hopefully.

"Speed up," Lt. Atcheson said. Because he had to say it.

There was a great deal of conversation among the guys as to whether Squid got captured or killed. Chum said he thought Squid was wounded during the run, which didn't ultimately answer the question.

It didn't matter a whole lot as far as we were concerned. Squid wasn't coming back to our outfit.

It mattered even less to Colavito, or at least that was his posture. He was never a fan of getting overly sentimental about things.

"I saw him lying facedown, with a couple of North Korean guards standing over him. He was either dead, or very, very patient, but I couldn't say for sure which it was."

The time had passed when we could have done anything for Squid, beyond ending the war and getting him sent home.

Our first major operation to that end was a mass United Nations assault on the port of Inchon. It was called Operation Chromite. It was not the most swashbuckling assignment we'd ever had, but it was as vital as any of the others. We operated in service of a wide-scale landing of troops and equipment from various Army and Marine outfits, converging on the Korean coast from spots around the world.

Included in that group was the Fifth Marine Regiment, out of Camp Pendleton, California.

That was Duke's outfit.

As we were shuttled on the longest Korean trip of our tour so far, I couldn't get that thought out of my mind. We sailed from our comfortable Japanese retreat, west across the Sea of Japan. Then we headed south along the east coast of Korea, sailed around the southern corner of the peninsula, and north again along the Korean west coast.

Finally, we arrived at Inchon, before most of the landing craft and troops were anywhere near the place.

As we made our familiar progression, from APD to LCP(R), and got close enough to the harbor to swim in undetected, I kept myself fully engaged with the thought that Duke would have been coming in soon with the landing force.

It was now my duty to make this spot of the world safe, so that Duke could pass through unscathed.

To do for him now what I wasn't able to back in California, all that time ago.

Sorry, pal.

The tides at Inchon were the stuff of legend, which was one reason we were there to map things out, along with several other UDT detachments. The difference between low tide and high was over thirty feet. My job was to use my old skills to travel the length, breadth, and depth of the harbor, to find the exact right place for a ship to navigate its way in under any conditions.

All around me, guys were "tanking up" with the underwater breathing apparatus. Three tanks were already hulking up Colavito's famously broad back, and that was fine for him. He looked part shark, and he couldn't seem to hold himself back from diving into the water. He was still affixing his mouthpiece when he backflipped into the bay.

Other guys were anxiously doing the same, gearing up and flipping over to get wet and get working.

"Last time, Frew," Lt. Atcheson said. "Are you sure?"

He held up a tank and offered the mouthpiece to me like he was threatening me with it. Though his manner was the opposite of threatening.

"I'm as sure as I could be, sir," I said. As I did, I gestured in the direction of the seabed, asking permission to dive.

"Away you go," he said.

And away I went.

As soon as I was down there, I felt a massive sense of relief, of peace and control. This wasn't the first time I was filled with this sensation. As far back as I could remember, the atmosphere under the sea, more than any other, was the place that would wrap me in contentment. I had a huge gulp of air in my lungs to keep me company and my glass mask affixed to my face, giving me all the sense of rightness a creature without gills could ever hope for down there.

And in that situation, I didn't have to explain the thing that made me doubly, triply set against swimming with the tanks.

They terrified me.

I had faced crazy surf and unruly crosscurrents many times. I had swum through hailstorms of machine-gun fire, and with worlds exploding at my back. I had shredded my flesh on coral pinker and sharper than Colavito's tongue, and banged my head on underwater boulder formations that very nearly knocked me out cold.

But once I learned about acute oxygen toxicity, there was no way I was going to strap any artificial breathing aids to my body.

My lungs were my most treasured objects. I was willing to put my money and my trust in them, over the very real possibility of having them overload on compressed oxygen with me floating way at the bottom of the ocean.

If I was going to die from the hazardous materials we had to handle in this job, I would just as soon snack on a ten-pound cake of C-3 explosives, thank you very much.

At any rate, the fear raised my game, as it does. By this time I was closing in on three and a half minutes without surfacing as my top diving time.

This helped as we prepared Inchon Harbor for Duke and the rest of the incoming fleet. I tracked a good half mile of sandbars that were deep underwater but would absolutely ground almost any draft ship that came this way during even half tide. All along the route, I worked in tandem with Sheldon to tag the path with buoys, which would act as traffic cops when the force finally arrived to deposit our guys onto the beach.

It was something of a reward when we were called back out the following day to witness the overwhelming sight of the flotilla of naval vessels arriving on the horizon, making their way into the shore. We were told we might be needed to clear a mine here or there, or unfoul any ships' propellers that got into difficulty. These were, no doubt, specialties in our UDT bag of tricks, and we would have been glad to help out.

But as we bobbed there on the swells and watched ship after ship sail in unimpeded to deliver the goods, it felt more and more like we were simply being properly rewarded for this job and all the others we had performed, largely undercover, out of the way, in the night.

We were appreciated, was the message. And the message was appreciated in return.

Here's to you, Duke.

CHAPTER TWELVE

Mines and Yours

Dear Ma,

Here's how to think of it, because it's the truth: My job here is the same as it has been for the past few summers. Lifeguarding. I guard people's lives, save people's lives.

Not just me, of course. I do have some help. You met my helpers, remember? We all save lives, on a regular basis, and that is the truth.

You would be proud of me. I know what you're going to say, that you are always proud of me, no matter what. But in this case, I mean specifically based on what I'm doing during my tour of duty. I think if you were aware of the tasks the guys and I carry out regularly, you would be mighty impressed.

I wish I could describe it to you, but I cannot. Not yet, anyway. But I promise I will reveal all, as soon as I'm allowed.

In the meantime, just go ahead and be mighty impressed anyway.

I have to keep this one short, Ma. They've got us wildly busy right now. But I'll write sooner next time. Writing shorter requires writing sooner, would you not agree? I think that's fair.

Soon.

Love,

Fergus

Well, it *was* true.

I said it was the truth, but I didn't say it was all the truth. Truth was a funny thing anyway. Was it necessarily a better thing than *some* truth combined with some consideration for loved ones back home? I would say that the second option was better. Consideration was clearly superior.

We were lifeguards and lifesavers. But we also carried guns and bombs and things. And we used them. Because sometimes we had to.

Mines. Mines were a good example of items that required some truth combined with some consideration. They also combined the lifeguarding and life-threatening aspects of the job we had to do in Korea.

The landing at Inchon was reported to have had the desired effect. But unfortunately, the initial invasion of the North Koreans down into the South was altogether successful. The Communist troops pushed whatever

174

American and South Korean resistance there was all the way down the peninsula, until the only real South Korean–held territory was a small semicircle in the southeast known as the Pusan Perimeter. By inserting troops on the west coast, halfway up the country, General MacArthur had figured to cut the territory and supply lines in half. So those troops were now fighting their way inland.

Our vagabond ways were only getting more dramatic, as our orders were now to come back down the coast, around the tip once more, and up the east coast to a port called Wonsan, near to where we had our first semi-successful raid after our arrival.

Wonsan was seen as an important piece of the overall strategy to retake the territory from the North. It was sort of diagonally across from the port at Inchon, where we had deployed all those troops, and it was reasonable to assume they were headed up there by now.

But they would need naval support from the harbor.

Problem was, the harbor was literally bursting with more mines than anybody had ever seen. It was like a giant gumball machine with killer gumballs. The Navy had first sent a flotilla of minesweeping ships to clear them out, but the situation was so dire that two of the ships, the *Pledge* and the *Pirate*, had already become victims of the mines themselves. Both were now sitting at the bottom of the sea.

So when minesweepers weren't up to the task of defeating this genuine sea of mines, who did they call?

I don't need to exaggerate the seriousness of the dangers involved. When we first arrived on the scene, along with four or five other flat-bottomed boats full of frogs, all we could do was creep gently into the harbor, trying to assess what we were up against. Several destroyers were anchored in the outer harbor, just floating helplessly, waiting for a resolution.

We crept along at about two knots, with Dover and Dogfish hanging over the front ramp, acting as minesweepers.

"I don't think the boat is gonna do it, Lieutenant," said Dogfish. "There's just too many of them. We'll need to go down there and get them ourselves."

The lieutenant let out a huge sigh on our behalf.

For our part, we had already broken into our two-man teams to get suited up. Nobody was feeling particularly brave, but we knew what we were there for, and we were prepared to do it.

Troops were progressing across the rugged terrain, all the way from the west coast. If we didn't clear this east coast port for their expected support, they would be walking into a slaughter.

The whole operation was like being charged with electrical shocks, such was the tension. My team was Dover and me. We swam forward, in the direction of the beach, parallel with all the other teams, carefully identifying the location of each individual mine. Every time one of us spotted one—floating as they did about five feet beneath the surface and anchored to the bottom with a metal cable—the other would submerge, get underneath it, and use wire cutters to release the mine. Then, ever so gently, we would tow the individual mines to a spot just beyond the edge of the inner harbor. More Frogmen waited out there, to tow the mines to the outer harbor for disposal by the sailors at anchor. They were shooting the mines with their onboard cannons.

Bu-hooom!

Bu-hoom!

Booom-bu-hoom-bu-hoom!

It was nerve-wracking, feeling the explosions of mine after mine while we continued to hunt for new ones in front of us. But it was the safest way to go about it. And it occurred to me that to the North Korean army, wherever they were, this must have sounded like we were already assaulting the beach.

This was the longest time we had spent on a daylight operation in hostile waters, but we did have the security of knowing there was a substantial fleet behind us that would pummel any troops foolish enough to come into Wonsan just now. Our work was the opposite of how we usually did things, sweeping mines instead of planting them, watching daylight turn to night.

Until eventually, there were no more mines to find.

The fleet of ships remained anchored in the outer harbor for the night, and we went out and joined them aboard our APD. We were all exhausted enough to sleep through the fight, even if the fleet had decided to assault the harbor right then.

Fortunately, they did not.

Less fortunately, we woke to the news that we were required to have a quick bite at dawn and then saddle up once more, taking the LCP(R)s right back into Wonsan Harbor to do a final recon of the waters before the fleet moved in for real.

So in we went, happy to have a less tense, less demanding task at hand after yesterday.

"You . . . are . . . kidding me," Lt. Atcheson said as we cruised to a near stop, and then an actual stop quite some distance from shore.

"What, did they *grow* back?" Colavito said in astonishment from the bow of the boat next to the lieutenant.

The harbor was just about as filled with those killer gumballs as it was the day before.

"They came back," the lieutenant said. "Under cover of darkness, under our very noses. They re-mined the whole place."

I don't know how we mustered the energy, other than having no other choice, but we went right back to the same job all over again.

Just before night fell once more, when we were being hauled back up into the boat . . .

Bu-boom!

There was an ear-shattering explosion not more than a hundred yards along the line from us. Another boat, an LCP(R) just like ours, had hit a mine. Another team, not so different from our own, had been instantly obliterated. Pieces of that boat shot high into the air, out to sea and onto the land. Pieces of boat, pieces of men, landed in the water all around us, and in the boat with us.

There was a flurry of activity aboard the overseeing craft. For a moment it seemed like they were reacting to this tragic event, but they had apparently already been in motion. We could see landing craft of every description being dropped onto the sea and filling quickly with troops. They were heading in as we were heading out.

Big cannons aboard the ships started firing booming shells, over our heads and onto the land beyond Wonsan Harbor.

This was happening. They would not wait one minute longer.

Over the course of the next two months, we were worked so hard that sometimes I thought I could go on a deep dive and just never come back up again. Like some kind of mythical sea creature.

Or like Duke.

Mostly we stuck to our specialty of quick nighttime raids that created mayhem for the North Korean supply lines. We also did much scouting and mapping of harbors in preparation for American and UN invasions.

Probably the most satisfying day, but also the saddest, was when we were called into another minesweeping situation. A third sweeper had gone under, not long after the *Pledge* and *Pirate* disasters. We pulled twenty-five sailors out of the water that day, reinforcing my claim to Ma about the lifesaving.

Unfortunately, a number of those sailors were no longer alive when we fished them out.

Then on Christmas Eve, 1950, we got probably the biggest emergency callout of our entire deployment.

The United Nations troops had been routed by the North Koreans and were making a fighting retreat cross-country. Like the famous British evacuation at the Battle of Dunkirk ten years earlier, there was a desperate call to get to the port of Hungnam and rescue the men so they could live to fight another day.

We arrived on December twenty-fourth in the middle of that evacuation. We fought through every type of warfare imaginable, plucking guys right out of the water and nearly sinking our own LCP(R) in the process of ferrying them out to larger ships. We did this over and over throughout the day, holding out for as long as the effort could, with the North Koreans closing fast.

American destroyers, cruisers, and battleships pounded the countryside beyond the port, in order to keep the enemy away. They did it until it was no longer feasible.

Then we got our orders to do what we could do better than anybody else.

The port was absolutely packed with American and United Nations supplies, stuff that would keep the Communists in good shape for quite some time going forward. The thought of the opposition staying healthy and strong on *our* rations, while killing us with *our own* arms, was something galling to contemplate.

So it was time for the Frogmen to see that didn't happen.

The LCP(R) ran all the way in and beached like the famous scenes of the landings at Normandy. The whole bunch of us ran full tilt and straight as arrows through the water, up the beach toward the warehouses and sheds and even railcars that were sitting there packed to the gills with our stuff.

Armed with tons of plastic explosives and detonator cord, Dover, Colavito, Lt. Atcheson, Crayfish, Shellfish, Dogfish, Chum, and yours-truly-Frogus fanned out evenly across the harbor front. We had strict instructions to wire up as much as we could in fifteen minutes, then leapfrog ourselves right back up that waiting ramp to the boat. At the fifteen-minute mark, the LCP(R) would reverse right out of the harbor, and if we missed the boat, we really *missed the boat.*

It was without question the coldest and most

miserable fifteen minutes of my life. Being underwater was no comparison to the miserable, rain-driven air of a Korean December. I was certain I felt rain pellets go up under my eyelids and down into my skull.

It was terrifying. And thrilling.

When I had wired up everything explosive I could manage, I spun and beelined it for the beach and the boat, at precisely the same moment that everyone else did.

That was a well-trained crew.

And as promised, the pilot backed the landing craft out of the shallows, turning it into the driving tide right on the button.

I knew, because I checked the great watch my mother had given me.

When we were back out, not yet dry but at least safe on the deck of the destroyer, we all counted down together. It sounded like the greatest Christmas carol ever croaked.

"Three! Two! One!"

Nothing happened. I nearly choked on my own tongue.

"Will we try TWO again?" Baccala called out, and as we yelled "TWO!" the biggest—no the BIGGEST, biggest—most glorious Christmas light show of all time exploded right there across our vision. Everything in the port of Hungnam shattered and burnt into history.

I knew then what *smithereens* were.

They sent us back to Japan for some well-earned rest. And after the holidays, they sent us to Pearl Harbor to teach the rest of the world what we knew.

And to do some surfing. The surfing in Hawaii was a dream.

Well. To be honest, it wasn't *that* much better than the surfing in my own backyard.

Then a couple of months later, they sent us back to my own backyard. Coronado, California.

You know, Duke, I did what you said. I saw the world.

And I am happy to say, the world was still waiting for me, right here. Right where we started it all.

About the Author

Chris Lynch is the author of numerous acclaimed books for middle-grade and teen readers, including the Cyberia series and the National Book Award finalist *Inexcusable*. He teaches in the Lesley University creative writing MFA program, and divides his time between Massachusetts and Scotland.

12/19